The man was stunning. He turned Jason mute.

Despite his huge dark sunglasses and his very strange wide-brimmed hat. The hat reminded him of something from a Renaissance painting, with a square brim that was scrolled over on both the left and right ends, the stovepipe squat and flat at the top.

In spite of the almost silly-looking thing, he still froze the words in Jason's mouth.

He was taller than Jason, a bit broader in the shoulders, but trim and well built. His peach polo shirt did nothing to hide that. Nor did the form-fitting khaki slacks, and Jason blushed when he realized his gaze had been drawn to the promising bulge of the guy's crotch.

When he looked back up, the man seemed to be staring, even though Jason couldn't tell for sure with those oversized sunglasses.

Then the man said a single word in a voice that sounded like music. "*Bellissimo.*"

WELCOME TO
DREAMSPUN DESIRES

Dear Reader,

Love is the dream. It dazzles us, makes us stronger, and brings us to our knees. Dreamspun Desires tell stories of love featuring your favorite heartwarming heroes, captivating plots, and exotic locations. Stories that make your breath catch and your imagination soar.

In the pages of these wonderful love stories, readers can escape to a world where love conquers all, the tenderness of a first kiss sweeps you away, and your heart pounds at the sight of the one you love.

When you put it all together, you find romance in its truest form.

Love always finds a way.

Elizabeth North

Executive Director
Dreamspinner Press

B.G. Thomas

THE NERD
AND THE PRINCE

PUBLISHED BY

Published by
DREAMSPINNER PRESS

5032 Capital Circle SW, Suite 2, PMB# 279,
Tallahassee, FL 32305-7886 USA
www.dreamspinnerpress.com

The Nerd and the Prince
© 2018 B.G. Thomas.

Cover Art
© 2018 Alexandria Corza.
http://www.seeingstatic.com/
Cover content is for illustrative purposes only and any person depicted
on the cover is a model.

Paperback ISBN: 978-1-64108-054-5
Digital ISBN: 978-1-64080-531-6
Library of Congress Control Number: 2017917867
Paperback published September 2018
v. 1.0

B.G. "BEN" THOMAS lives in Kansas City with his husband of more than a decade and their delightful dogs Sarah Jane and Oliver. He is blessed to have a daughter as well as many extraordinary friends.

Ben loves romance, comedies, fantasy, science fiction, and even horror—as far as he is concerned, as long as the stories are entertaining and about *people*, it doesn't matter the genre. He has gone to literature conventions his entire adult life where he's been lucky enough to meet many of his favorite writers. They have inspired him to create his own stories; it is where he finds his joy.

In the nineties, he wrote for gay adult magazines but stopped because the editors wanted all sex without plot. "The sex is never as important as the characters," he says. "Who cares what they are doing if we don't care about *them*?" But then he discovered the growing male/male romance market and began writing again. He submitted a novella and was thrilled when it was accepted in four days. Since then the romantic tales have poured out of him.

"Leap, and the net will appear" is his personal philosophy and his message. "It is never too late," he testifies. "Pursue your dreams. They will come true!"

Website/blog: bthomaswriter.wordpress.com

By B.G. Thomas

DREAMSPUN DESIRES
GETTING HIS MAN
#48 – Getting His Man
SMALL-TOWN DREAMS
#66 – The Nerd and the Prince

Published by **DREAMSPINNER PRESS**
www.dreamspinnerpress.com

This one is for Elin Gregory.

What a dear friend,

I've dropped in on her online without warning or preamble more times than I can count, and she is always available for me. She is friend and advisor and guide and researcher and very good at getting my butt out of the fire. She is an amazing historian and helps with stuff I didn't even have a clue I needed help with. And this book was really one of those. Without her I do not know how real Monterosia would have been. And gosh, so much (of course) was never even able to make it to the printed page. Maybe there needs to be another story about this wonderful kingdom? I hope you think so.

But meanwhile, Elin, I love you more than you can know.

And I thank you so much for making this novel and so many others possible!

Home is behind, the world ahead,
and there are many paths to tread
through shadows to the edge of night,
until the stars are all alight.
~ J.R.R. Tolkien, *The Fellowship of the Ring*

Chapter One

A BIG storm had blown through the night before. Jason Brewster had lain in his bed listening to it as it went from a distant rumbling to loud rolling booms that shook the house and the windows in their panes. But he'd loved storms since childhood, when his father had explained that if you counted the seconds between the flash of lightning and the thunder, you knew how many miles away the storm was. As an adult, Jason wasn't sure if that was true, but the idea had delighted him as a kid.

He'd decided not to research it to see if it was true or not despite the fact that he was a research kind of guy. Why mess with a fun childhood belief? Did it matter if it was true or not?

But even better were his mother's stories that storms were caused by ancient gods like Thor and Indra and Lei

Gong and Taranis, and of course Zeus and Jupiter (who, wow, were the same god with two different names!). She said all the booming and shaking and flashing were the gods kicking up a fuss because they were angry that people didn't worship them anymore or believe in them or even remember who they were.

"I know who they are!" cried Jason Evander Brewster, who was named after not one, but two mythological heroes. He knew it too. Because hey! He'd looked the names up in the library where his mother worked. She'd told him tales—he wanted more. Looking things up was fun!

"And that's why you'll never be struck by lightning," she promised, and he would smile and go to sleep peacefully on even the stormiest of nights. Not just because he'd taken enough interest in finding out about the ancient gods—she told him they loved him for it—but also because he'd read articles on the odds of being struck by lightning, and it was pretty darned unlikely. One in 700,000 in the US in any one year. *Pretty* darned good odds!

"You are *such* a nerd," said his twin sister, Daphne, who was also named from mythology. "Who even looks stuff like that up?"

He decided not to be upset by what she said. Maybe he was a nerd. But then *he* was sleeping at night, and a thunderstorm could send her running for their parents' room.

Their mother's name was Iris, and she was named after the goddess of the rainbow because *her* mother loved the old stories as well and had been the one to pass on that love to her daughter.

Some people in town swore Grandma had been a witch, and the idea that she could have been was just one more delightful "what-if?" in Jason's life. What if she was? He didn't know. He had almost no memories of her, as she had died when he was very little. And Mother! Why even though she went to the little United Methodist Church every single Sunday without fail, she didn't have a single picture of Jesus, not one cross or crucifix, in the house. There were, however, little statues of Jupiter and Juno and Diana on her bureau. They were the only things in the house he and Daphne weren't allowed to touch growing up, especially the coins and flowers and candy or cookies or even bread she left there before them. Once in a while, she even left a glass of her honey mead.

This only fueled their childhood imaginations all the more.

"What if Mother is really a dryad?" Jason might wonder aloud while alone with Daphne by the creek behind their house, or late, late at night under the covers with a flashlight.

"Or a naiad!" Daphne might suggest.

"Nah. A dryad," Jason would argue. "She loves the woods but doesn't like swimming so much."

"What if that's because she would turn back *into* a nymph if she got in the water?" Daphne would counter.

"*Wait!*"

Daphne waited.

"What if Daddy is really a satyr?" Jason asked, eyes widening at even the slightest possibility that such a thing could *possibly* be true.

Ideas like that would cause them to dissolve into giggling fits, for it was one thing to picture their mother as some kind of earthen spirit, but it was another to imagine their father, delightful as he was, as a drunken lustful woodland god.

Although he and Mommy did like to make honey mead, and sometimes they'd drink it and get giggly themselves and look at each other the way he and his sister looked at the big jars of candy or the triple sundaes at the soda shop in town. This made Jason and Daphne cackle all the more.

"*Ohhh*…! I've got a good one! What if Daddy *isn't* our daddy! What if Zeus appeared to Mommy as a silver swan or a shower of gold and *he's* our real father?"

The idea that they, two skinny little kids from Buckman, Missouri, might be the children of the king of the gods—like Amphion and Zethos—was quite marvelous and enchanting. But it also made them feel guilty because they loved their father and didn't *really* want to belong to anyone else. Not even a god.

They liked the idea far more that there were miracles, because that is what their mother called them. "My little miracles." Because they had come late in her life. In fact her doctor told her that she most likely would never have children. "So we never used protection," she would tell them, although it wasn't until they got a little older that they figured out what that meant. "And I prayed. Prayed for a miracle. And Diana gave me two!"

It was with pleasant memories like these that Jason had slipped off to sleep the night before as the storm began to distance itself. He'd slept like a baby. The morning broke on a gloriously sunny spring day. Daphne called him as he came downstairs to start the coffee (the one thing everyone would want) to let him know that one of the big trees in the park, one of the really big ones that had been around when their grandparents were kids, had fallen in the storm.

"Oh… that's too bad," he said and tried to imagine the sight, because he couldn't jump in his car and check himself. He had The Briar Patch to open. Which is why she'd called him with the news.

"But at least it was the one on the southwest corner," she replied.

The one the kids couldn't climb because it had a sheer trunk, and its lowest branches were a good ten feet off the ground.

"I'm so glad it wasn't the Giving Tree," Jason said, referring to the tree the two of them had named because it had given generations of children so much fun, with its wide-reaching low branches that any kid could climb. *And* after the book by Shel Silverstein, which their mother had read to them countless times and which they both loved so much. He still did, and in fact he had an autographed copy sitting on a shelf he'd found on eBay and built into the headboard of his bed.

Oh, his mother loved books. She'd been a head librarian her entire life, until she finally stepped down from the position only last year at Father's urging. He wanted to travel. Of course, that didn't mean she wasn't at the library all the time anyway. She couldn't stay away. And she passed her love of books on to her children. Dad loved books as well. And thus, The Briar Patch, Jason's part used bookstore and part diner—serving breakfast and lunch six days a week.

Reading and cooking were two of Jason's greatest pleasures.

Cooking! Every kind of omelet imaginable, along with breakfast burritos and fruit-filled pancakes and biscuits and gravy (his Grandma Higgs had taught him how to make them) and chicken salad sandwiches (totally from scratch) as well as tuna salad (he used canned for that) and patty melts and Reubens to die for. And that was only his standard fare. At least once a week he'd fry up a couple of chickens (Daddy's mother taught Jason her version, which was better than Grandma Higgs's, although he would never tell his mother that) or a big pot of stew or make a big roast with all the trimmings. Sometimes he'd experiment and try something new by searching for recipes on the internet. A cute guy named Todd he knew in high school had shown him that cyberspace held a rich collection of recipes. Funny that he knew you could use the internet to find out how to blow the dust from his laptop's cooling fans and that Febris was the goddess with the power to cause or prevent fevers, but he hadn't thought to use it for recipes before then. But he hadn't realized he liked cooking before then either.

He envied Todd sometimes. When his buddy had gone to seek fame and fortune in Kansas City, Jason stayed behind with the internet. Todd was helping manage a big-deal restaurant called Izar's Jatetxea, while Jason's fame in Buckman was his quiche. He found he was really good at it, although baking sweets, for some reason, eluded him. Especially pies and cakes. He could never figure out why his ham 'n' cheese quiche and his Tex-Mex quiche and even his pear and Roquefort cheese quiche always turned out perfect, but his pumpkin pies ended up soupy or solid or rubbery. Not to mention his lemon meringue.

Which is why the fresh pies he served were made by Wilda Chandler, a family friend.

But of course even greater than his fondness for cooking was his love of books. He *loved* to read. Anything and everything.

Fantasy because of those god stories with which his mother had filled his childhood ears. And of course J.R.R. Tolkien's *Lord of the Rings* trilogy. And only slightly less loved were *The Chronicles of Narnia* by C.S. Lewis. The Deryni series of novels by Katherine Kurtz, *The Belgariad* by David Eddings, and *Outlander* by Diana Gabaldon.

Then there was science fiction. *Dune* by Frank Herbert. *The Foundation Trilogy* by Isaac Asimov, Arthur C. Clarke's Space Odyssey series, nearly anything by Ray Bradbury or Connie Willis.

So many authors! Guy de Maupassant, Barbara Kingsolver, W. Somerset Maugham, Daphne du Maurier, and O. Henry. Mark Twain.

So many books! *The Stand*. *Charlotte's Web* and *The Color Purple*. *The Handmaid's Tale* and *The Joy Luck Club*. *Eagle of the Ninth* and *Maurice*.

The Front Runner by Patricia Nell Warren had changed his life. His mother had fought tooth and nail to get the book in the library. He started reading it for that reason and had been stunned to see it was the love story of gay men. It was the book that gave him the courage to come out, first to his sister and then his parents—none of whom had been surprised.

"Oh come on," Daphne had said, rolling her eyes. "I'm your twin. You think you could keep that from me? You think I hadn't figured that out? I knew that before I knew you were a nerd."

"Then why didn't you say anything?"

"Silly! Because I thought *you* had figured out that *I* had figured it out!"

So many wonderful, *wondrous* books. Between his mother's stories and his lifelong collection of books, oh, how his imagination soared!

Well, there were actually three things he loved. Because he also loved *getting* people to read.

Which was why he loved The Briar Patch.

"Don't you think opening a bookstore in Buckman is a little iffy?" Daphne had asked when he'd told her what he'd decided to do with the house their great-aunt had left them. "It isn't like our fellow citizens are very literary."

He'd shrugged. "If I'm going to live here, then I better do something I enjoy."

"But—"

"No buts," he cried, holding up a hand. "My mind is made up!"

"You are *such* a nerd," she said, laughing.

"Like you haven't already established that!" he said, joining in.

He was lucky his nerdhood hadn't made him any enemies in school. No friends, but no one who hated him. No bully to pick on him or throw the books he *always* carried into a mud puddle. No dreaded wedgies.

But no friends. Daphne was in fact his best friend. Of course, in a graduating class as small as theirs, there wasn't a whole lot of choice. But his love of books hadn't made him the guy everyone wanted to hang out with.

And then there was writing. He'd found a driving need to tell his own tales of passion and adventure. He'd even had a couple of his gay romances published through a company called New Visions Press. How shocked and stunned he'd been when he sold that first novel only a few weeks after submitting it. The second novel had even done well on Amazon. Gail Southgate, the owner and executive director of the publishing company, had even written him recently and asked when he might be writing them something else.

It was a happy-sigh moment.

So that was four.

Cooking, Reading. Getting other people to read. And writing.

No, wait! He also loved encouraging other people to write. To set pen to paper and tell *their* stories. Several evenings a week, The Briar Patch was open to groups who needed a place to meet. One of them was his twice-monthly writers' group, with members ranging in age from sixteen to seventy-six. He'd been happy that the group he'd started was getting people to express themselves. In the tiny boring town of Buckman, population 2,749, where almost nothing ever happened.

Despite its size, however, he loved his town. As small and out of the way as it was.

That didn't mean he didn't want more, though. Dream of it. Wish for it.

Adventure. Something more exciting than the town's three-lane bowling alley or one of two bars or the new(ish) movie theater. Heck. They were lucky to have a movie theater!

But wouldn't it be nice to see some of the places his books and imagination took him to? Iceland or the Taj Mahal or Khajuraho temples in India or the Forbidden City in China or the Eternal City of Rome?

Italy! Home of the gods.

Or to see the Parthenon in Greece....

But in the meantime, there was The Briar Patch.

He and Daphne didn't talk long that morning. He had to prep for the breakfast customers, but she did let him know she'd be in to help when he opened. *After* he cleverly reminded her that Monday was the day Tom Rucker came into the Patch before going out on his weekly run. Tom was an over-the-road truck driver and recently had been flirting with her, and she, well, she had been flirting back. Which made Jason happy. She hadn't shown any interest in a man in he didn't know how long.

An hour after that, he was serving a surprisingly large crowd.

Apparently quite a few people had gotten up to go see the fallen tree—there wasn't a lot to do in Buckman—and look around to see what other damage had been done.

Except for a four-by-four block area that was out of power because another tree had fallen, luck had shone down on the citizens of the town. He actually had some people waiting to be seated. He'd taken care of that by having Daphne set up a couple of card tables on the porch. In the end, Jason had actually run out of eggs and bacon. A first in a long time. Despite that, everyone had been in a cheerful mood, and not one customer had complained about eggs cooked wrong (while they'd lasted), biscuits too hard, grits not buttery enough (considering there was a stick at every table, and they therefore could have as little or as much as they wanted), or coffee too weak or strong.

Wonderful.

And yes, Tom had come in, and he was hunky and had moved to Buckman last year from a neighboring town. He owned (or was buying) his own truck cab and would pick up trailers all over and take them wherever they needed to go. It was risky going into business as an independent trucker these days, but Tom was trying, and Jason could only respect that. And he sure made Daphne smile.

Gorgeous. Not really Jason's type—Tom didn't read and loved country and western music—but he was gorgeous. And like Jason, Daphne needed some loving. It was good to see one of them getting it. Or maybe soon, anyway.

Then during the cleanup—two hours where no meals were served, although you could come in for a slice of fresh pie (today's were apple, coconut cream, and raspberry)—Jason got his favorite kind of customer. In this case, two high school boys actually looking for a book. Well, one of them was. He'd read the book *All American Boys* by Jason Reynolds and Brendan Kiely for one of his classes and been surprised that he loved it. He looked nervous to even admit it, and his friend had carefully busied himself looking at some joke books while they talked.

"Do you have anything else like that?" the kid asked. "It seemed so *real*."

Luckily, even with his limited shelf space, Jason thought he had a thing or two to offer and suggested them. The award-winning, provocative coming-of-age novel *Monster* by Walter Dean Myers—about a teenage boy in juvenile detention and on trial—and *Speak* by Laurie Halse Anderson, even though it had a girl protagonist. He thought maybe the boy could handle it. Jason had a sense of such things.

Then to his surprise the other boy admitted he liked *To Kill a Mockingbird* and wanted to know if the chick who wrote that wrote anything else. Sadly, Jason had to admit that the only other book Harper Lee ever wrote was *Go Set a Watchman*, which was more an early draft of *Mockingbird* than anything else. The boy still showed interest, so Jason made a snap decision and ran upstairs and got his own copy. He could always get another.

And he'd gotten someone to *read*.... He'd called Daphne with the news.

"That's my brother," she said. "Spreading nerditude to the masses."

"Sis, I'm just happy people are still reading books at all."

That was so important to him. The Briar Patch had started off as a used bookstore. But Daphne had been right. Not enough people in Buckman read. Not even with the neighboring communities. But it was also Daphne who'd suggested he make the Patch a part-time restaurant as well. So he'd given it a chance—after all, there was a kitchen right there, set off to the side. And he'd already been pretty much been selling more coffee and muffins baked by Wilda than books. To his happy surprise, people came. Between the books and the food he prepared, he could pay the utilities and keep the doors open.

Lunch that day was brisk, and he had no real problems. Why, he'd even gotten his sister to run out for more eggs.

And it was at lunch that Mrs. Halliburton, easily eighty years old, asked him if he knew anything about whoever it was who had bought the house behind the Patch.

He had to fight to keep his mouth from falling open. "What?" Someone had moved into the house behind his? Why, it had been empty for… what? Two years at least. No one had lived there since Kathy and Melissa, a lesbian couple he'd befriended and who'd invited him over at least once a week so they could play cards and watch movies and sometimes get high. Well…. They would get high, but not him. Drugs always spooked him. He'd seen them mess up too many people. He would have a beer with them, though. More than one.

But then they got into a huge fight, actually tried to kill each other, and the cops came, and one of them went to prison (although for something completely different). The other went and worked at a hospital and became a licensed medical assistant and met a man—a surgeon, in fact—and the last Jason heard, they'd gotten married.

It had made him sad that they didn't have a happily ever after. The couple of years they'd been together had given him a different dream than ancient gods or being a famous writer. Their love had given him the hope that he might find love with a man. Their horrid fight and explosive breakup—something that neighbors in all directions for one or two blocks had witnessed and judged—had all but crushed that hope.

As if cursed, the house had been empty ever since.

Mrs. Halliburton and her two friends looked at him over plates of biscuits and gravy and big mugs of coffee laden with real cream and raw sugar.

"I—I didn't know anything about it."

How could he have not known?

"I hear whoever it is has already moved in," said Mr. Ainsley, the widower of Mrs. Halliburton's best friend, Ella Ainsley. A rumor said that Mrs. Halliburton and Mr. Ainsley were courting, although it wasn't obvious to Jason.

Jason looked eastward, as if he could see through the windowless dining room wall to the tiny house behind The Briar Patch. How in the world had he not seen anyone move in? After all, what did he, or anyone, have around here *to* see? Wasn't that why he was being asked about the place? Anyone moving to Buckman was news, but someone moving quietly into a long-empty house? That was *big* news around these parts.

He turned back to his three guests. "I... I...." He blushed, thinking how stupid he must look. "I haven't seen anything. My bedroom window points that way, and I haven't see any lights."

Mrs. Halliburton rolled her eyes with much exaggeration. As if she *did* think he was stupid. At least Mr. Ainsley and their companion, Ethaline Merton, who was easily old enough to be the mother of the other two, only looked at him sadly and without judgment. Correction. Mrs. Merton was looking off into a corner near the ceiling. She had a sort of smile on her face as if she was seeing something no one else could. Who knew? Maybe she was.

"Hey, Jason" came a call from behind him. It was Sheriff Ryan—complete with his cowboy hat. "Can I get some more coffee?"

"Sure, Sheriff. Be happy to." He turned back to the elderly trio. "I'll keep my eyes open and let you know if I find out anything. Can I get you some more coffee?"

Both Mrs. Halliburton and Mr. Ainsley shook their heads. Mrs. Merton muttered something about "seeing" or "scene," maybe, and smiled beatifically. Jason didn't know what to say about that and simply went to the kitchen to fetch the coffee.

He was too busy to give much thought to someone moving into the little house.

Not very much.

Luckily, lunch cleanup was easy. Near everyone had wanted the special, the homemade cheesy meatloaf with real mashed potatoes, or one of his quiches, of course. He'd already washed what he could as he'd cooked, so there was no big deal with the pots and pans. *And* he had a dishwasher, something that would have been ridiculous for only him in this two-story house. But with the restaurant, it was a godsend. And his dad had gotten it for him for a steal at one of the endless auctions around town. Who knew such a small town could generate so much *stuff*?

After he locked up, he went upstairs and took a long bath in his beloved old-fashioned, and quite huge, claw-foot tub and read the newest romance by Jude Parks. He'd wondered why his great-aunt, who was a tiny woman, had put in such a large tub, but he loved it even though he was a pretty small guy himself.

Timothy Jeske, the high school quarterback, had told him—when no one was around—that he was as slim as Sally, Tim's… girlfriend? Jason had never been able to figure out what Sally had been to Tim in those days, the two of them were so on-again, off-again. He suspected that the "on" part had to do with the fact that Sally was so pretty and Tim was so hot, and naturally everyone expected them to date. But if Tim was serious about her, why had he told Jason that he was as pretty as Sally was? Something that had both excited and embarrassed Jason at the same time.

"As pretty as a girl," Tim kept saying and looked at him in ways that made Jason's spine near melt. Tim had also been the one who had taken his virginity. Hadn't done a very good job of it, either. He had the angles all wrong and hadn't understood that you had to be a little more careful back there than with the anatomy he was accustomed to. But in the end, what Tim was doing to him had gotten just good enough that Jason had been willing to do it again when Tim had come knocking at the door—the front door—of his parents' house.

The second time had been much better.

As well as the fiftieth time. And the times after that.

But then Timmy (that was what Jason called him when they were alone) had gone off to the University of Alabama on a scholarship, something that had made him a Buckman hero—small-town boy making it big—but had come back two years later after a terrible injury that had made it impossible for him to ever play professionally. He'd come home in defeat—sullen, angry, and not all that different from Mrs. Halliburton, who was bitter (it was said) that her family company had folded. And once, at one of the town's only bars, Tim had called Jason a faggot in front of his friends when Jason had stopped by with a rare desire for a beer. He didn't drink that much, and a six-pack would have sat in his refrigerator taking up room he needed for the Patch. Thus his visit to the out-of-the-way bar with the hilarious name (to Jason anyway) of Duck Inn Bottoms. "Duck Inn" because… well, he had no idea. And "Bottom" because it was located at the far end of town, which was also the lowest point and because of that had flooded a time or three through the years. But oh, the funny things you could think up with a bar with that name.

Everyone had laughed.

It had hurt, of course. Pissed him off, in fact. How could the boy who had been his first—who had kissed him hundreds of times, who'd told him he kissed so much better than Sally, who had made love to him by the river under the stars—call him a faggot?

So later that night he called Tim (who was staying with his parents while he "looked for a house") and told him that he better never do it again.

"And if I do?" came the slurred reply.

"Why, I just might tell Sally"—who it seemed was Tim's fiancée, now that he was back in town—"about that peculiar noise you make right before you cum. You know…." He screwed up his face even though Tim couldn't see it. "Ah! Ah-aw aw *ah* aw aw! Ah-aw aw aw aw—*eeee! eeee!*—*aaaaaawwww!*"

There was a slight gasp from the other end of the line.

"I bet she knows that sound, Timmy. If she's good enough to make you *make* that sound, that is…." It was a mean thing to say, meaner than he was wont, but he was pretty fuming mad.

"You… you wouldn't."

"*Try* me, Timmy…."

Timmy didn't.

Jason was pretty sure he'd been in love with Tim. And he'd been silly to think that he wouldn't have to be a secret any longer once Tim went away to college.

That Tim would see being gay didn't have to be a big deal, and they could be a couple.

It didn't happen.

And now Jason was just lonely.

He knew there were other gay people in town. And "bachelors" who lived together but never ever showed any affection in public. Everyone knew, but no one said anything above occasional whispers. Buckman wasn't going to burn crosses in anyone's yard for any reason, and that was one of the reasons Jason *did* love his hometown. For such a tiny place, its people were rather open-minded, and most of them had even voted for Obama, although they were on the fence about Clinton—a woman—running for president.

Jason's loneliness was the worst of it. He could be satisfied with only seeing the Parthenon on the poster in his bedroom. He could keep Rome as a secret wish. He could spend the rest of his life in Buckman.

But oh, how he wanted to be loved.

After his bath he tried to read some more, and then Gail Southgate's words came back to him, as they had more and more lately. "When might you be writing us something again? Your stories are just what we look for. You are a true romantic."

A true romantic. For whatever good that had done to help *him* find romance.

But maybe that was what his books were for. Maybe he was living vicariously through them? He thought about Sam Eldridge, the strapping hero of his latest book. He was a museum curator who had been opening some recent Roman acquisitions when quite suddenly a statue of Mars had come to life. It was humorous, he hoped, and sexy, again he hoped. Mars did not understand that he couldn't just smite anyone he wanted, and modern technology was putting him into mourning seeing a world that didn't need gods anymore. Why not…?

Jason was booting up his computer when he looked over at the one statue in his home, a young man leaning back in the wings of an exceptionally large eagle. It was Ganymede, of course. And the eagle was Zeus, who had fallen in love with a male mortal and swept down from Olympus and carried Ganymede back to the home of the gods to be his cupbearer and forever lover. It was a tale Jason never stopped sighing over.

But then something else caught Jason's eyes.

A light.

He got up and approached the dresser and statue and looked out the back window, then let out a little gasp. A sigh, really. The little house behind his. There was a light in the kitchen window.

A light!

There *was* someone in the house.

Jason trembled. He didn't know why.

He smiled, only vaguely unaware that he was doing it.

But then there wasn't much to get excited about in the tiny boring town of Buckman, population 2,749.

Where almost nothing ever happened.

After that there was no writing about Sam Eldridge or a sexy Roman god.

His imagination was on whoever was in that house.

He had a pretty good imagination.

Chapter Two

THE house was not what Amadeo Montefalcone had
been expecting.

The photographs from the internet had made it
seem much nicer, otherwise he and his brother would
never have picked it. And even though he'd known it
was small, to find out that his childhood bedroom was
bigger than the entire house had been a *bit* of a shock.
There were houses in villages he visited—something
the people loved about him—that were bigger.

The distance between Buckman and the Kansas
City airport was also unexpected. How far Buckman
was from *any*thing in fact. All those American movies
made it look like all you had to do was jump on the
convenient bus that stopped off at any and every small

town, and in no time you could be on your way to New York or Chicago for the day.

But God, America was *big*. He'd known that, of course. Intellectually. But the reality was… well, almost too much to take in. His entire country was smaller than the smallest state, not even twice the size of Washington, DC, which wasn't even a state at all. A "district." And district meant something else where he had grown up as well.

The drive from the airport to Buckman had been a surprise, even though his brother had laid out everything for him, step by step. It took him two hours, and the road was lonely in the dark. The only thing he could really see by the light of the moon were crops and fields and boring, boring, boring.

It was the kind of road you heard about alien abductions occurring on….

Two hundred kilometers. That was longer than his entire country from one long end to the other… by almost four times!

And his country was gorgeous. The "miles" he was driving were boring, flat, nothing!

To add insult to injury, the car his brother had selected for him was something called a Toyota Camry. About the most indistinct car he'd ever seen in his life. How would he be able to distinguish it from any other?

Another culture shock was the ride *into* town. First, Main Street was wider than the little highway he'd driven all those kilometers on. Why would such an old town need such a wide street? You could park a semitrailer truck lengthwise across Main and still have plenty of room to go around. At least he found his new home quickly, although he hadn't been able to tell a thing about it in the dark. He let himself in—he found the key "under the mat," apparently an American custom—and he couldn't help but wonder why anyone bothered to lock their houses if everyone knew where to find the key. He wouldn't be doing that.

The electricity was on, which was good, and the mattresses, if not an actual bed, had been delivered, which wouldn't have happened if the key hadn't been in its accustomed place. The water was running too. All good. But the floor...!

The next morning he found he didn't like the color of the house at all. Wasn't even quite sure what it would be called. Tan? Peach? Putty? Faded-bloodstain brown? *Che schifo!* He wanted it repainted. Soon!

Blue. Blue sounded good. A really pretty royal blue, maybe. Or a deep sky blue. Maybe a turquoise. Something people would compliment him on and....

"You have to blend *in*, Amadeo," Cristiano said. "Not stand out. You're used to standing out, my brother. You want to hide from the world, then you better hide. The color might not be all that pretty, but people will drive right by and not give it a second glance."

And of course, Cristiano was right.

So for now the house would stay *schifo*—gross.

But then there was the matter of the floor. The living room floor. It sagged. Badly. As if it was rotting or something. A big dark spot in the ceiling on that side made it look like there was a leak in the roof. How in the world was he supposed to get this fixed? Without asking his brother what to do to get it done? Hadn't Cristiano done enough already? Enough to be called a traitor, maybe?

Amadeo knew he had to think for himself. He wasn't a stupid man. He'd accomplished amazing things.

He just didn't want to do what his father wanted most.

Floor. Living room floor. That's what he needed to focus on. And how to get it fixed.

So Amadeo got on the internet. Facebook, in fact. He found a swap-and-shop page for Buckman. Pressed the button to join. He could maybe place an ad? Or get pointers on how to find someone to do repairs on the little house....

Such a little house.

God, he wished he could call his brother. But it was seven hours ahead in Monterosia and not a good time to call him. Their calls needed secrecy.

He liked the back patio. If that was what it was called. It had a roof to protect it from the elements and the sun, which was good. A little picket fence surrounded it. Plantings, some of them pretty big, would help conceal him. Because right now being concealed was the name of the game.

Amadeo had thought hiding in this little place in the middle of nowhere would be easy. He'd underestimated the invasiveness of the media. What a surprise that had been. Maybe it shouldn't have been. But it was!

The night before he had gone to Walmart. Shopping. He'd never really shopped before outside of a loaf of bread here, some flowers there, some fresh Roma tomatoes elsewhere. The people liked it.

The store was a *huge* place, though. There was nothing like it in Monterosia. Wondrous and ghastly at the same time. And strangely exciting. Shopping. How amazing it was to take a shopping cart—something he'd never used before in his life—instead of a basket and go up and down the aisles, perusing the wealth of items available: from tennis shoes to towels to alcohol to pet supplies (should he get a dog? A cat?) to house paint to eyeglasses to guns (imagine—to be able to buy a gun so easily!) to groceries to clothing of every imaginable variety.

He was looking for a few things. A fan. A lampstand. Things for the bathroom. He'd walked through the electronics department, where there were several big flat-screen TVs playing all at once. The house had one of those, but he thought he might get a DVD player and some movies. A show called *Longmire*. Maybe.

And then suddenly, right there on screen after screen, was a story about him. A picture of him in the garden dominated the space. He was smiling, laughing, brown hair swept back, but part of it still falling over his forehead, blue eyes sparkling. It was said that his eyes could make any woman's heart race. Not at all what he wanted.

In the photograph, he was wearing a white shirt and a blue European suit jacket. Casual. Yet still *elegante*. The screen made his image life-sized. It was like looking into a mirror.

Amadeo had fled the place. Left everything in the shopping cart behind.

Had anyone seen him?

Worse, he got to the parking lot and almost panicked. He couldn't find his car. Except for the plethora of pickup trucks, the cars all looked the same. Then he remembered he could press a button on the key fob to make the car horn beep so he could find it. A complete relief.

Hours later, when the crew of *Today's Entertainment News* didn't show up, it occurred to him that no one had been paying attention to the television. No one had looked at him twice. No one was looking for him here in Smallville, USA. No one had given him the slightest bit of attention.

And he was hungry. He needed, at the very least, the groceries that had been in that shopping cart. And the spatula. And the frying pan. The butter. Walmart's selection had been horrible in some ways, almost gluttonous in others. Most of the pasta looked normal, although there wasn't much of a selection. But they'd had butter. Organic even. What Americans called food items that were *real*.

Amadeo looked at the sagging floor. Sighed.

Well, he had a refrigerator. Along with a few other things that had come with the house. An old couch, not horribly uncomfortable. A small table—big enough for two, although of course he was only one. But being one was part of the reason he was in this country.

There was a bookcase with two books in it. A book called *Rubyfruit Jungle*, odd title, and one called *Down from Olympus*. A good sign he supposed. That's what he was in a way, right? Down from Olympus?

"*Accidenti!*" he shouted to the empty room. "Have I made the biggest mistake of my life?"

There was a little *bre-leep* from his laptop—the internet was something he'd made sure he had before he got here!—and when he looked, he saw he had been accepted as a member of Buckland Swap and Shop.

Hmmm....

Allora. What are you going to do about it?

Place an ad, he thought.

He had a fork. He had a refrigerator. He even had some paper plates.

Maybe I should have a floor that doesn't sag.

He kneeled before the laptop on its simple wooden coffee table. He *had* a coffee table. If not for the cigarette burns, it might have been cute.

Could I sand that down? Or get a handyman to do it? No. I will do it myself.

He opened a new post and typed.

WANTED. HANDYMAN.
General handy work. Possible roof.
Sagging floor. Simple plumbing.
Please email me at

Amadeo paused. Thought about the email address.
He'd almost typed in the one he'd used for years.

Merda! He was no good at this. But he was going
to have to be. He changed "possible roof" to "possible
section of roof" and then added the email address
Terranova1989@gmail.com.

He posted the ad along with a picture of the house.
Done. Simple.

He stood. Looked at the floor. Turned to the kitchen.

The refrigerator was in dire need of cleaning.
Would Walmart still be open? He shrugged. He could
find out. Amadeo's stomach growled, reminding him
he needed food even more. He would go see.

Another chirp issued from the laptop. He looked
down at the screen. He'd gotten an email. He toggled
over to Gmail, and yes, there it was. An email from a
Timothy by Demand titled I Am a Handyman.

He opened it.

> Hey there. My name is Timothy
> Jeske and I can do everything you say
> you need done in your ad. I'm good
> and available most of the time. Give
> me a call.

So Amadeo did. Got Timothy by Demand on the
phone in two rings and, hearing the deep masculine
voice, imagined him as an older man, maybe in his

forties, overweight, wearing a flannel shirt. It was probably unfair, but he could only go by what a lifetime of American movies and television series had shown him. He couldn't help but wonder if Timothy would chew tobacco and show his butt crack when he was working under the sink.

Turned out Timothy could come over at nine the next morning, and that was good. Amadeo could get the floor taken care of as quickly as possible.

Signing off, he almost told Timothy that his name was Amadeo, but then he remembered it was seriously time to start using the name Cristiano had come up with for him. He was no longer Amadeo Montefalcone. He couldn't be. He'd left that behind. Run away from that.

So now he was Armand "my friends call me Adam" Terranova.

Terranova. He'd liked that immediately.

New land.

And he was certainly in a new land.

Amadeo's—*Adam's*—stomach growled again.

Food.

He'd go to Walmart. Fill his grocery cart. It was time to get serious. He was starting a new life. This could be exciting.

And then, quite unexpectedly, he *was* excited. He felt better than he had in days. Weeks, really. Months?

He was starting an adventure. And while it had actually begun two days and several flights earlier, two of them on small private planes (one of them terrifying) crisscrossing Europe before heading to the United States, he now felt that the first *real* step was the one out his front door.

Adam—he said the name out loud, "Adam"—opened his door. To the north was downtown, and to the south, the Walmart on the edge of Buckman's city limits, where he was about to go. Which made him nervous. Despite the fact he was headed to such an ordinary place, a line from one of his favorite books occurred to him: "It's a dangerous business, Frodo, going out your door. You step onto the road, and if you don't keep your feet, there's no knowing where you might be swept off to."

Adam's heart skipped a beat. He smiled.

His door. This was *his* door and *his* house, and not something his family had lived in for hundreds of years. It was all his. Suddenly the house didn't look so ugly anymore.

It was home.

It was the heart of his new life.

Who knew what was going to happen?

And right now? Well right now, he stepped out the door.

Chapter Three

SOMEONE knocked at Adam's door promptly at nine the next morning—impressive—and he slipped on his overly large sunglasses and, as an afterthought, the wide-brimmed traditional nobleman's hat of Monterosia. Passersby in a grocery store probably would never recognize him. Most people had never heard of Monterosia. Even with the recent news stories. But the less chance there was of him being recognized, the better. And besides he'd already checked; it was going to be a very sunny day.

He opened the door.

Timothy Jeske was not in his forties, was not chewing tobacco, and was not wearing flannel—in fact, he wore a black T-shirt that had the mysterious 5FDP written across the front. Adam couldn't begin to guess what that might mean. Timothy also did not show his butt crack when he looked under the sink.

Adam guessed him to be in his midtwenties, probably hadn't shaved in a few days, and while not exactly overweight, he was a bit stocky, maybe twenty-five pounds or so extra. Nice-looking enough, Adam supposed. But not his type either.

He liked his men slim. Slim almost to the point of girlish, but still a man. No body hair. He figured his tastes in masculinity had been hardwired from a childhood where his only chance to see a naked man was the ancient statues of mythical heroes. Lean like Hermes, Discobolus, or Achilles and sometimes, surprisingly, even Apollo. Of course, Ganymede. Not the statues of Hercules or Zeus or Atlas. Trim, but still muscular, with high round asses. Maybe those statues were why the size of a man's penis meant little to Adam compared to a lovely round bottom.

No sooner had he decided that he wasn't really attracted to Mr. Jeske than he realized the handyman was looking at him, it seemed, with interest. *Sexual* interest.

Not my type, he reminded himself, even though it had been a long time since he'd been with another man, and a morning of making love could be wonderful.

Except it wouldn't be making love, would it? It could be nothing but a dalliance. And part of moving to America was that he wanted more than that. *Craved* it. Was tired of trysts in dark alleys of Rome or Paris (or during his secret trips to Amsterdam) with men whose shadow faces he could barely see and who he worried might give him some social disease for his trouble.

That could lead to him having to explain how he'd contracted such a condition, and if from whom, it might come out that he'd gotten it from a man. And Adam was not ready for his family to know he was gay. Adam was pretty sure they weren't ready either. He had no idea how they would react. Sure, his father had stated his support for GLBT rights and had already voiced his approval for same-sex marriage before Parliament. But would he feel that way when it came to his eldest son? Somehow, with Amadeo Montefalcone's responsibilities—with what was expected of him, the very least of which was producing an heir—he suspected his father's support might not be so forthcoming.

So he had pretended his entire adult life to be what his father, and his country, wanted and needed. Even though it left him cold and alone. He'd had the love he so desperately needed only once—in college abroad—and the touch he wanted only rarely, and equally in secret.

Oh how he longed for human touch. Even Timothy's lingering touch when they shook hands sparked something inside of him.

Timothy did look muscular. His shoulders were broad. The way his jeans hugged the full mound of his ass was very promising. Would it be so bad to seek a few pleasures of the flesh? An *avventura*?

Maybe not....

But *after* the work was done. *Don't mix business with pleasure.* He made that decision while the handyman was under the house and not looking at him with those knowing, hungry eyes.

As it turned out, though, the prognosis was not so dire. Timothy would have to tear up the rotting section before the damage spread to the bedroom, then lift up that part of the house and replace a beam. And everything he needed was available at hand.

"I can get most of it at Burstyn Lumber, which isn't even a half mile down Main, and the rest of the stuff locally as well. Probably even the 4x12." Timothy wiped some mud off his cheek. "I can also lay down some new carpet from the Home Depot in the next town over and get rid of that mildew so it won't smell so bad."

"How long?" Adam asked, dreading the answer. Where would he stay? The local Best Western? Where some high school boy or girl would be manning the front desk and glued to social media and far more likely to recognize him than shoppers at Walmart or Timothy by Demand, smiling handyman, ready to recarpet his little home.

"I'm sure I can have the floor, and *maybe* the section of roof, done by dinnertime tomorrow."

Adam gawked at him. Tomorrow? He'd been sure it would take Timothy weeks.

"It ain't Buckingham Palace."

Adam didn't know what to say. No. Indeed not.

"I mean it's a small place. Really small."

Nor Castle Monterosia either.

"And—" Timothy turned and pointed at the porch. "—you got two front doors."

Indeed he did, and it was a feature he didn't really understand. There was the obvious door that faced the street. And if you stood looking at it, then turned directly left, the house jutted out from the porch and there was a second door there, facing south—a door to the bedroom. "Yes," Adam said. "Unusual, isn't it? Why do you need two doors on the front of a house so small?"

"Don't know," Timothy said, squinting into the morning sun.

Adam asked *the* question then, and Timothy answered with a price, and Adam agreed, totally unaware if it was a fair amount or not. Why had he even asked?

"You ain't from around here, are you?" Timothy by Demand asked.

Adam looked at him. Shook his head.

"It's your accent."

Of course. God.

"You're from *Boston*, ain't you?" Timothy winked knowingly. "I *know* accents."

Ma dai. Apparently not, thought Adam and almost burst into laughter. Because Boston was over six thousand miles from the land that had given him his accent.

He almost told Timothy that yes, he was from Boston. Born and bred. But "oh what a tangled web we weave, when first we practice to deceive." He figured he'd better do what Christiano had told him and stick with the persona that had been created for him. Leave as few lies as possible.

"Rome," he said.

"France?" Timothy asked, growing more unattractive. Even for an avventura.

"Italy," Adam said.

Timothy winked. "I was just testing you," he said.

Adam winked back, then realized the handyman couldn't tell through the large concealing sunglasses Adam wore.

"It's also that big hat," Timothy said, and Adam reached up, unthinking, and touched its very wide brim. "No American dude would be caught frigging dead in that. What are you supposed to be," Timothy scoffed, "one of the three musketeers?"

"It's the sun," Adam lied, instantly forgetting his conviction. "I'm sensitive. I—I burn easily." And realized he would have to add it to his fictional biography.

"Makes you stick out like a sore thumb."

Adam went wide-eyed and was glad Timothy couldn't see. Standing out was the last thing he wanted to do. He fingered the brim again.

"Here's a pointer," Timothy said, resting a hand on one hip. "Either the man wears the hat, or the hat wears the man."

Ah yes. Now this he understood. But when he'd looked at himself in the mirror the first time wearing it, he'd thought *he* was wearing the *hat*. Timothy didn't think so.

"Get you a baseball cap," Timothy said and pointed at his own, worn backward.

Adam stared at it for a moment, then thought, *of course*. In just the last couple days—including the airport!—how many men had he seen wearing *just* such a hat?

Why, it seemed like almost all of them.

"What kind should I get?" he asked.

"You like the Royals?"

Once more Adam did a double take. *The Royals?* Was Timothy a fan of royalty? Adam couldn't breathe for a second.

Timothy must have sensed his confusion. "You know... baseball?"

"Baseball?"

"The Kansas City Royals?"

Adam did laugh this time. "Ah! Baseball. America's favorite pastime."

Timothy shrugged. "Some people would say it's football."

Adam *didn't* make a comment about *that* sport. Or why it was called *football* when the ball, in America, was only actually kicked maybe eight or ten times in the entire game. He'd been warned Americans were sensitive about that issue. So he just nodded instead.

"You ever seen a baseball game?"

Adam shook him head. "No."

"Maybe I can bring a six-pack by later. There's a game on. I can explain it to you."

Hmmm…. Maybe. Could be fun. If he was going to hide in this country, he should probably be familiar with the things its people found important. And God… there was a devil whispering in one ear of the fun he could have with this man. Even now, the stranger's eyes were making a hungry offer, and Adam *was* hungry. There were times he felt as if he were starving.

"Excuse me" came a voice that made them both jump, and when Adam turned, he froze.

And beheld one of the most beautiful young men he'd ever seen in his entire life. Slim but not skinny. Adam could see a nicely developed chest even with the loose blue casual dress shirt. He had an almost boyish short haircut and skin like creamy marble. But it was his riveting big blue eyes that almost took Adam's breath away.

"*Bellissimo*," he whispered, and all thought of Timothy the handyman vanished without a trace.

THE man was stunning. He turned Jason mute.

Despite his huge dark sunglasses and his very strange wide-brimmed hat. The hat reminded him of something from a Renaissance painting, neither fancy nor overly adorned, with a square brim that was scrolled over on both the left and right ends, the stovepipe squat and flat at the top.

In spite of the almost silly-looking thing, he still froze the words in Jason's mouth.

He was taller than Jason, a bit broader in the shoulders, but trim and well built. His peach polo shirt did nothing to hide that. Nor did the form-fitting khaki slacks, and Jason blushed when he realized his gaze had been drawn to the promising bulge of the guy's crotch.

When he looked back up, the man seemed to be staring, even though Jason couldn't tell for sure with those oversized sunglasses.

Then the man said a single word in a voice that sounded like music. "Bellissimo." Or at least Jason thought that was what he said.

"I'm—I'm sorry?" Jason somehow managed to say. He knew he should know what this word was—bellissimo—and what it meant. But if he had ever known its meaning, it was whisked away from his memory like a puff of smoke in a sudden breeze.

The moment was so powerful (later he would not for the life of him be able to describe it) he almost dropped the spinach artichoke quiche he was carrying.

After all it *was* hot. The heat *had* begun to radiate through the pot holders.

And the man was staring.

Tim Jeske cleared his throat. "Ah…." He gave a curt nod. "Brewster." And when Jason's high school secret lover spoke his last name, it proved to be the magic word to break the spell that had seemed to fall over both him and the otherworldly stranger.

"*Scusami*," the man said hastily, yet still in that musical tone. "I…. Excuse me." He stepped forward and looked at what Jason was carrying.

Jason held it out. "I b-brought you a… housewarming present," he said.

He'd woken thinking about who might live in the little house. He'd dreamed about it. In one, it had been an eagle that had taken up residence, and it flew from the back door of the house, over the little fence that surrounded the little patio, and across the back lawn, alley, and Jason's yard. Right through Jason's window it had flown, and somehow that window had been wide and open and inviting to the mighty bird. His window didn't open that way, but in dreams it didn't matter, did it?

Only one shiver of fear shook him as the big brown eagle zoomed toward him on widespread, silent wings. It took Jason's shoulders in its talons, bigger than a man's hands, and then lifted him high, high, and higher into the evening sky, leaving first Jason's home and then the entire town of Buckman below, spread out like a patchwork quilt.

Jason was not afraid. Instead he felt glorified. Picked. Chosen. Powerfully sexual. He'd woken disappointed. He stumbled to the bathroom, where he prepared himself for the day.

And he found his thoughts wandering to the tiny little house across the alley behind The Briar Patch, and he couldn't help but wonder who was living there—

(An eagle!)

—and how he might find out.

If only to be able to tell Mrs. Halliburton and her friends.

(Except a part of him, a deep-inside part, whispered that he should keep that to himself—to be *his* secret.)

Looking out his bedroom window at the putty-colored house, he wondered…

Who lives there? A man? A woman? A couple? High school sweethearts with their first place together? Maybe newlyweds?

Would there be children running and screaming? He hoped not. Life had been so quiet and peaceful (lonely) in the time he'd lived here in this house his great-aunt had left him and his sister (who had no desire to live here at *all*) when they were in high school and that he'd moved into soon after graduating. With hopes of finding a boyfriend to share it with, of course. Or at least of bringing a man home now and then. But that hadn't happened, had it?

He remembered it was trash day, and he hauled the bags on the back porch to the big blue city waste container and stopped and looked across the alley and pondered.

Someone old? Someone young?

Straight...

...gay?

While he made quiches for the day, Jason wondered. And then it hit him.

A housewarming present. He would take one of the quiches over as a housewarming present. One without meat in case whoever lived there was a vegetarian.

And now? Now his hands were starting to burn!

"Can I put this down?" he asked. "It's hot, fresh out of the oven!"

"Oh! *Scusi!*" The man leapt forward with such grace and took the hot piedish, along with the pot holders, and said, "What is this, please?"

What is it? He didn't know? "Quiche," he replied.

"Key-sh?" the man asked.

"Quiche." He'd never heard of quiche? "It's made with eggs and cream, and then you add other stuff." Jason swirled his finger over the dish as if he were mixing it. "This one has cheese and spinach and artichoke."

The man raised it to his face and drew in a long breath. "It smells wonderful."

Oh, his accent! So beautiful. Italian?

"You give this to me?" he said in that musical voice.

Jason nodded and found himself blushing for some reason. "Yeah. It's a housewarming present."

"House... warming?" was the reply.

Goodness. He didn't know what a housewarming present was? Jason turned and pointed across the alley. "I live in the house behind you," he said and pointed. "And I was just welcoming you to the neighborhood."

"Ah! *Bello! Grazie! Grazie mille!* Thank you so much!"

"You're welcome," Jason said, and he fell in love with the man's voice.

"Is it for eating now or waiting until it cools?"

Jason laughed. "You can eat it now if you want."

"*Beeee-llo!*" He smiled and it was perhaps the most beautiful smile Jason had ever seen. "Allora. So, then… you join me? We…." He sighed and even that was lovely. "*Come si dice*…? How do you say in English? We could serve it up?" Then he smiled again, and Jason's heart nearly—

A loud throat-clearing noise made both Jason and the man jump.

It was Tim. God. Jason had forgotten he was there. "I guess I'll go get the supplies."

"*Accidenti!* I am *so* sorry Mr. Jeske. Please. You join us?"

Jason felt his heart drop. The last thing he wanted to do was share this beautiful man with Tim Jeske.

"Nah." He seemed to be giving Jason a look with daggers included. "I don't like quiche." He made a nasty face. "Besides, I promised you this tomorrow."

"No!" said the man. "*Basta!* I won't hear another word. Join us!" Then, "Dai! You are right!" He looked at Jason. "This *is* hot!" He turned and took the few steps to the porch and rested it on the railing.

"Don't burn yourself!" Jason cried.

"Almost!" came the man's answer, and he smiled and sucked the heat off his fingers. It was perhaps the sexiest thing Jason had ever seen in his life.

Get a hold of yourself!

Once more Tim cleared his throat. "No. I gotta go. Stuff to get." Then, giving Jason dagger eyes again, he said, "Maybe later? The game?"

"Game?"

"The *baseball* game?"

"Oh! Of course. Maybe. Maybe…."

Tim snorted and walked off. Jason couldn't have been happier.

The man turned and picked up the quiche. He grabbed the handle on his screen door with one finger and opened it. "*Prego, entra*," he invited and nodded at Jason.

It wasn't hard to figure out what he'd said, and smiling, Jason went into the little house.

Chapter Four

THE inside of the house brought up a lot of memories, but goodness.... How had that floor sagged so much in just a few years? He glanced up and saw the dark stain in the corner of the ceiling. Oh. Gosh. Had Kathy and Melissa had problems with the roof?

"Ah. Yes. That is what I am hiring Mr. Jeske to fix."

Jason blushed. He hadn't meant to stare. Would...? Had he been rude? And hell! He didn't even know his new neighbor's name.

"This way?" said Mr. Beautiful. "We go to safer place? How about my piazza? It is nice, I think."

Piazza?

The piazza turned out to be the little back patio. But it had a nice sloped roof, which looked new. Jason's host set the quiche on the table and then motioned to one of the two chairs at the small table. Of course Jason tripped over his own feet as he went to the table, and could he have done anything worse? When Jason moved to sit, his host held the chair for him and then pushed it in. Goodness. No one had ever done that for him.

Jason's new neighbor then took off his ridiculous hat and swept into the house, grace personified. Jason looked at the hat for a moment, and then a grin spread across his face. Why, it reminded him of the Munchkin coroner's scrolled hat from *The Wizard of Oz*. He almost laughed. But God! What if his host saw him smiling this way?

Mr. Beautiful returned bearing a wedge-shaped knife. There was a slight breeze, and his dark hair, flipped in long bangs across his forehead, ruffled slightly in the breeze. Sexy. Jason didn't know why, but sexy. The hair, not the knife.

"We will have your quiche. Is how you say it? Correct? But first, I have been most rude. I have not introduced myself and have not asked your name, signore." With that he actually clicked his heels tightly together, gave a barely perceptible bow, and said, "I am Adam Terranova. I have come to your fair village from Rome and am eager to know your country. Welcome to my home."

Jason smiled. He couldn't help it. This was like something out of a movie or fairy tale. And he liked it. A lot.

"I'm Jason Evander Brewster," he replied, compelled to say his whole name.

Adam Terranova smiled then in a way more beautiful than any yet. Jason's heart skipped a beat. "Ah," Adam said. "You are named for heroes from antiquity. Were only I so blessed."

As Jason looked on, Adam cut the quiche into pieces that were about half the size Jason would serve his customers. He was surprised but didn't say anything. Maybe Adam had already eaten. And it was a little odd to be sitting here ready to eat with a complete stranger. Why, they had barely exchanged names.

But then came the coffee. It was another surprise to say the least.

The cups were small. *Really* small. They almost reminded him of the cups he and Daphne had used when there were playing house as children. And they appeared to be only half-full of coffee.

"Sugar?" asked his host, and before Jason could reply, *almost* dumped a heaping teaspoon of sugar into the cup. He stopped at the last possible second. A few grains fell in anyway.

"Ah, sure," Jason replied, although it was more from being stunned than anything else.

"Cream?"

Jason shrugged and then stared as Adam poured cream until the small cup was filled to the brim. Then Adam prepared a second cup the same way. He then sat down opposite Jason and smiled again.

"*Prego! Cheers. Mangia!* Eat up."

Jason took a sip of the "coffee" and nearly choked. Not only was it sweet, but *God*! Strong! Holy *crap* it was *strong*.

"Ma dai! Are you all right, Jason?"

Eyes watering, Jason held up a hand, almost afraid to look up. Thank goodness, he somehow managed not to spit it out. "I'm fine." He managed a weak smile. "S-sorry. I've just never…. Your coffee. It's different."

Adam looked stricken. Even wearing those glasses. So… what? Disappointed? "I am so sorry! *Scusa!*"

Jason shook his head, all but horrified now. Geez, what an impression. What must this man think of him now? "I'm fine. I feel like such an idiot."

"No, No! You are not an idiot. Perhaps I am. I knew you Americans drank your coffee weak."

God. He looked so upset. *What have I done?*

"And you drink it in such abundance. I could not believe how much people drank on the planes I took once I got to your country. And in the airports. It amazed me!"

Jason laughed, thinking of how he rushed about in the mornings refilling his customers' cups. "Viva la difference?" he asked.

Adam smiled again, and God it was beautiful. Maybe the bad moment was over? His teeth were perfect and so very white. "*Viva la differenza.* Long live the difference. Indeed. Would you like me to get you something else? Something less… strong?"

Jason shook his head. "Not really. Although you could get me some water."

"*Certo!*" Adam said and was up and away—and those words filled Jason's mind: Live the difference. Gosh! Then Adam was back with a glass and a bottle of water.

This time he did something else. He took off his sunglasses. At last Jason could see his eyes. So blue! So *very* blue.

They were the most beautiful eyes Jason had ever seen.

And Jason was lost.

IT was the second time his new neighbor—Jason; he liked that name very much—got that sudden… lost expression on his face.

Oh God! He's recognized me.

Breathe. Keep calm.

"Are you all right, Jason?" he asked, hoping his fears weren't true.

Jason's cheeks pinked. He looked away. Then slowly looked back. Oh, those eyes. Those beautiful eyes. He could fall into those eyes. He wanted to kiss them.

"I… I…. Sorry." Jason looked away once more.

Adam reached out, almost touched Jason's hand. Didn't. He was not sure if that was all right here. He'd been told that the way men touched each other, kissed each other's cheeks, in Europe was considered taboo in America.

Unmanly. Gay. *Finocchio. Frocio.*

"It was the coffee is all," Jason said and would not meet Adam's eyes. Too bad. He wanted to look into those eyes.

"Jason. *Sicuro?* You sure?"

"Your eyes," Jason whispered. Or at least that's what Adam thought he'd said.

"My eyes?"

Jason looked at him. Opened his mouth. Closed it. Turned crimson and looked away again.

"Jason?"

"They're beautiful…," he whispered.

Whispered. But Adam heard him. Felt *his* cheeks warm up. *He thinks my eyes are beautiful?*

"Thank you, my new friend," he said. "I find yours to be beautiful as well. Bellissimo."

"B-bellissimo?" Jason said.

Adam nodded. "It means beautiful."

"Then when you said…."

"Sì?" Adam prompted. "Yes?"

Jason shook his head. "Nothing," he said in that same quiet voice. He looked up at Adam through heavy-lidded eyes. It was a look that contained all kinds of possibilities. Might this lovely young man be gay? Could the fates have been so kind? To meet someone so soon?

There is Timothy Jeske.

Adam shook off the thought. How could he even think of Timothy by Demand now that he had met Jason Evander Brewster?

Well, at least you know that Timothy loves men. Or at least fucks them.

And while a fuck sounded good, hadn't he come here for more?

Jason was still looking away, and Adam had no idea how to go on from here.

Put him at ease. Don't scare him off.

"You know, in my country," Adam said, "it is not… taboo for men to regard something as beautiful. We look for beauty. Cherish beauty. Celebrate it. It doesn't make us…." He almost said gay. But the word lodged in his throat. He couldn't say it. He couldn't say it because, because he *was* gay. He'd run away from the home and the family he loved, the country he cherished, and the responsibilities he'd been born to fulfill. He'd abandoned all of that to live a gay life where perhaps—perhaps—he would find love with another man. Could he now act, in any way, as if being gay were a bad thing?

No.

"Where I am from, a man can notice the beauty of another man's eyes. It doesn't make him… any less masculine."

"But… I *am* gay," Jason said.

Adam froze for just a moment. How remarkable. "What a pleasant surprise," he said.

A tiny smile flicked the corners of Jason's mouth upward. He had a lovely mouth. "Pleasant?" Jason asked.

Adam nodded. His heart began to beat faster. "*Sì*. I came from so far away. And I was nervous. You know? I hear America is good for homosexuals. You can get married. Not so where I live. You have Gay Pride. We've never had a Gay Pride. No parade. No celebration with Patti LaBelle and Ariana Grande and the RuPaul. You have programs like *Unbreakable Kimmy Schmidt* with the hilarious Titus Andromedon."

Jason's lovely blue eyes were growing a bit wide.

"But I also see that some of your politicians do not like gay men and women, even when their son or daughter or sister is a gay or lesbian. That you have places that serve chicken that fire gay employees. And madmen with machine guns who kill dozens of people in a nightclub. It is very mixed messages, sì? You know?"

But now Jason's eyes were even wider, and Adam wasn't so sure that was a good thing.

"Perhaps I have placed too many acts in a comedy?" he asked.

"Huh?" Jason asked, clearly confused.

"You do not know this saying? *Fare troppi atti in commedia.* To make too many acts in a comedy. See?"

Jason did not look like he saw.

"A play has three acts, usually," Adam continued. "To have too many means to try and say too many things at once. I should have simply *said* that, as a man in a new land, a land with the good and bad—" Now he did reach out, take a chance, and touch Jason's hand. "—it is a pleasant surprise to receive as a 'housewarming gift' this quiche. And to find that my new neighbor is gay. It is *very* nice. I hope that we will be friends. It would be nice to have a gay friend. Especially one with such beautiful eyes."

That last may have been too much, but then that was who he was. Often going just a few steps too far. His father would shake his head, his brother roll his eyes, his mother shrug and say, "He is who he is." And the people would love him for it.

But what would Jason say?

Then Jason turned a dazzling smile on him, and it took Adam's breath away, and he thought maybe he had gone just far enough.

"Maybe now we should eat? I hope my talking has not made it cold."

"Well.... We could always microwave it." Adam could hear the reluctance in Jason's voice.

"Sorry, no microwave yet. So mangia. Dig in!"

They did.

It wasn't too cold. It tasted very good, but not quite what he thought it would be like. With talk of cream, he thought it would be sweeter.

"You don't like it?"

Adam looked up from the plate into Jason's very blue eyes. They showed concern. *Oh no!* Had he done it again? "No! No!" Adam said. "It is *delizioso!*"

Jason's eyes warmed again.

"It is just a little... saltier than I expected. We don't usually eat something salty for our morning meal." He took another bite. The combination of eggs and cheese and artichoke, with just the perfect amount of spinach, really was *very* good. "This reminds me much of something we call torta salata. Very close."

"Just less salty?" Jason asked.

Adam bit his lower lip. "Ah. No. We just wouldn't eat it for breakfast."

"What do you usually eat?"

"Sweets," Adam replied, and smiled. "Cornettos or crostatas or doughnuts."

Jason looked at him curiously.

"Cornettos are like a croissant, but smaller and not as buttery and has a glaze made with orange rind. A crostata is a tart filled with jam. And doughnuts are...."

"I think I know what those are. Unless they are different in Italy. Like the British call their cookies biscuits."

Adam laughed. It felt good to laugh. "Yes. I saw doughnuts at your Walmart. They seem to have *every*thing! I've never seen anything like it."

Jason rolled his eyes.

"What?" Had he said something wrong again? What was going wrong with his ambassadorial skills? His father wouldn't have been happy had this happened at home.

"Never mind. A subject for another day." Jason smiled.

Adam decided to go with it. He liked Jason's smiles. Took another bite. "This is what we might have for lunch. Eggs, bacon, sausage…."

"And pasta?" Jason grinned.

"Of course!"

"And tarta…."

"Torta salata," Adam corrected.

"Which is like quiche except…." The tone and the flash in his eyes spoke of teasing.

"One of my nannies once told me it was a way to clean out her refrigerator with whatever was on hand. Which Cook would never have said!" He laughed yet again, this time at the memory. Sagging floor or no, he felt good. When had he found such humor in such small things?

When had he last sat across a table from another gay man? Especially one who knew *he* was gay? The answer was a very long time.

"Cook never served what was left. She threw it away."

"Threw it away?" Now Jason's eyes were wide again.

Yes. Because there was no way she was going to serve royalty anything but the most gorgeous meals. He had found entire entrees in the garbage because it had bubbled over wrong or gotten just a bit too brown. It had bothered him more and more and more as a child, and he had gone to his father more than once about it. "There are hungry people outside these walls, Father," he'd said on one morning, tears in his eyes. "Looking for food in the garbage. While Cook throws away very good food!"

Fortunately Father had relented. Compromised, really. He knew Cook would never serve them anything that didn't look like it couldn't be photographed and put in a cooking magazine. But starting then, all leftover food was turned over to the palace servants on a rotating basis. A kind of year-round, revolving Boxing Day. He was loved for it. People who might have only ever glanced at such food now dined on it on a fairly regular basis.

"Well, she used to. Not anymore."

He'd gotten Nanny to bring him a piece of her torta salata. More than once. One time it was nothing but cheese and meat and basil in a crust. Delizioso!

"Anyway, we would have this for lunch and pastries for breakfast—"

"With coffee as strong as an elephant and as sweet as you," Jason said, and then he blinked furiously and slipped a hand over his mouth, his cheeks once more going red.

Adam burst into laughter, unable to be anything but pleased. Now if only Jason liked his coffee. *So* sad about that….

Jason gulped, his Adam's apple bobbing. "I…. Ah…."

"It is okay," Adam said. He took a chance and touched Jason's hand again. To his surprise, his new neighbor immediately turned it over so that Adam's fingertips now rested in Jason's palm. It was a wonderful

little shock to his system that—yet another surprise—
went straight to his cock. But did Jason mean to have
this effect on him? He simply didn't know American
ways. He met with ambassadors and dignitaries from all
over Europe, but rarely anyone from the United States.
Maybe men from America could do this publicly?
"Remember," he continued. "We are friends now. No
reason to be embarrassed."

He withdrew his hand then, denying the urge to
lightly stroke that soft palm. But God he wanted to!

"Would you like another piece?" Adam asked then,
for lack of anything else to say.

Jason shook his head. "I've got four more at home."
He pointed over the patio railing at his house. It was a
pretty, light mint green. Much nicer than the color of his
own place. "It's also my business. I serve breakfast and
lunch, as well as have plenty of used books for sale."

"Really?" What another delightful surprise.

"Sure," Jason said. "If you're free, come up anytime.
If I'm not serving at the time, there are always books."

"I love books! My shelves here are empty of but
two." This was delightful. What a coincidence. And
while shopping, he would have an excuse to talk to
this beautiful young gay man. Who knew what might
happen? And here he was worried about how he would
meet other gay men.

That was when he remembered Timothy the
handyman. Who wanted to bring over a "six-pack" so
that they could watch a baseball game. God. The moment
he'd met Jason, the tryst he'd entertained with Timothy
had been erased. Jason was not only beautiful and
sweet—he had brought him a housewarming gift, which
was not a Monterosian tradition—but he read. Timothy
thought Rome was in France. Then he got an idea.

"Jason, do you like the baseball?" he asked, crossing mental fingers. Hoping.

Jason gave a little shrug. "Sure. Around here going to see the Badger's play sports is about all there is to do. They're not bad either. Why?"

"The handyman…. He wants to come over and watch the game with me today. He is going to bring a six-pack. I think he wants more than that. I do not think I am interested. If I had a friend here as well, perhaps that would… how do you say? Defuse the situation?"

Jason's eyes went wide. It seemed to be a little quirk of his. A cute one.

Relax, Adam. You are not going to find love less than forty-eight hours after moving to a place where you can look for it. Life doesn't happen that way.

But still his breath caught, waiting for the answer.

"Why… sure."

He let out the breath almost explosively. God! Did Jason notice?

Jason chuckled. "So you don't want to be trapped alone with Tim Jeske, huh? I don't blame you. Although in another time and place in my life…."

Adam paused, waiting for Jason to finish his thought. Then he got it. "Oh! He is an old lover…?"

"I don't know if we were ever lovers. I was his secret, because he wouldn't want people to know he likes men. Or at least having sex with them. It was high school, and I fell head over heels for him, but it was only sex. He says he isn't gay. That he's… a little bisexual, maybe. That's what he *said*. But for a man who's only a 'little bisexual,' his libido never seemed to cool. Sure, he wouldn't bottom. But criminy did he love to suck…." Jason's eyes flew wide *again*, and he clapped a hand over his mouth. This time he turned positively crimson.

Adam fought not to laugh. It might only embarrass Jason more. He nodded instead. "I got you." But what he desperately wanted to ask was "Do *you* still like to suck cock?" He didn't, though. He'd been raised better than to be so crude.

He was struck then—almost hard enough to make him gasp—that he *could* be so crude if he wanted to. Not because this situation warranted it. No, he thought it would ruin the atmosphere they had created. But simply because he, for the first time, really truly had the freedom. The worst that could happen was that Jason would leave and not talk to him again—which admittedly was a pretty bad thing. But there would be no earth-shattering scandal. Nothing to rock the press. No reason for his father to come to him horrified at what he'd done. Nothing to hurt family or house. He had the freedom to do something distasteful.

For a moment he thought he might actually cry.

"Are you all right?" Jason asked, and of course those eyes had widened. Had they looked this beautiful yet?

Adam's smile came from the marrow of his being. "Yes," he said. "I am very 'all right.' I can't remember being so…. Feeling so…." Free? If he said that, what would Jason think? That he was weird? "I am good."

Jason's smile returned. "Good."

They looked at each other for what seemed an impossibly long time then. A time Adam was afraid to ruin by speaking.

A ringing phone broke their silence.

Jason looked down at his cell phone. "It's my sister," he said and picked it up.

"Hey, Daphne," he said. And once more his eyes went wide. "Oh shit! I'll be right there!" He jumped to his feet. "No, I mean it. Less than a minute. I'm that close."

He hung up without another word. "The Briar Patch. I'm late opening. People are waiting outside!" He pointed at the mint green house again. "I lost all track of time."

He looked around him.

"Here," Adam said and rose from his chair. "There's a gate." He went to it and opened it for his new friend. At least he hoped Jason was a friend. At least a friend.

"Thanks," Jason said and all but ran for it. Then he paused for a second. Stared.

Adam's heart seemed to stop.

"I'll see you this evening? For the game?"

And then began to beat again. "Yes. This evening."

Jason grinned. "Okay." He went through the gate and stopped again. "And if you want a book, just come on up. It'll be on the house."

Adam wasn't sure what that meant, but he nodded. "Mayhap I will take you up on it."

And then Jason ran, literally, across their mutual lawns and disappeared around the side of his house. The Briar Patch is what Adam thought he'd called it. Interesting name. He'd have to figure that out.

He sat back down. His eyes went to the "key-sh." He laughed.

Contemplated freedom.

And cut himself a second piece.

It was *huge*.

Chapter Five

"WHERE have you been?" Daphne asked as soon as Jason came around to the front of the house. Thankfully things didn't look as bad as he'd thought they might be. There were only two people standing on the ramp from the lawn up to the porch and front door.

He thought of Adam and blushed.

Adam Terranova. *New land.*

Daphne's eyebrows shot up. "Jason?"

He said nothing. As he unlocked the front door, he wondered why Daphne hadn't already done it. She had a key after all.

Jason turned to face his guests, two sisters in their fifties who came by about once a week. "Sorry Mrs. Clifford, Mrs. Livingston, for having to wait. Coffee is on me this morning." They smiled. After all, they could put away a lot of coffee. He was glad they always came together because he could never remember which one was which. If one of them ever did show up alone, he would be in trouble.

They sat, and Daphne all but chased him into the kitchen, where he grabbed a pot of coffee and two mugs.

"Tell me, Jason. You're blushing. Did you get laid?"

"*Ssshhh!*" he hushed her and went to the checkered-clothed table where his guests were seating themselves.

He poured their coffees and asked them how they were doing. He knew he didn't have to get cream. Neither took it.

They told him in great detail all about everything new in their lives. He was barely paying attention anyway. What he was thinking about was Adam Terranova's eyes. And his smile. His laugh. The way he'd touched Adam's palm and sent delicious shivers all up and down his skin and straight between his legs. He couldn't remember the last time a man—a real-life, right-there-in-front-of-him man and not Kit Harrington or Ryan Reynolds—had made him feel anything like this.

"Don't you think so too?" came a sudden question. He looked at the two ladies. He had no idea what they'd asked him. He smiled. "Oh yes," he said, and thankfully the bell over the front door tinkled and in came two more guests. "Good morning!" He held up the coffeepot. "Sit wherever you want. Coffee?"

Of course.

Back in the kitchen, Daphne was on him like a second skin. "Spill it, brother!"

"I might get burned," he replied and poured the contents of the near-empty pot into the next one— which made it dangerously full and yes, a possible scalding waiting to happen. He put the empty one into the Mister Coffee and started another pot with a filter he had already prepared.

"Jason! I know you. And I know you are never late. *And* I know by the look on your face that something has happened. *And* if you got laid then I want—"

"I didn't get laid, for God's sake!"

The bell over the door rang again. Did this mean it was going to be an early day?

Jason checked, and it was Sheriff Ryan. Two days in a row. Okay. "Coffee, Sheriff?" he asked from the door of the kitchen.

"You bet. And I already know what I want. A country omelet with hash browns."

"You got it, Sheriff," he said with his best customer-service smile. A glance showed that Mrs. Clifford and Mrs. Livingston weren't so thrilled that the sheriff had bumped himself to the front of the line. But hey, it paid to wear the badge. And it wasn't like they'd be delayed that much. He ducked back into the kitchen.

"*Jason*!" Daphne hissed.

"I have customers!" he hissed back. But then he saw Adam's eyes in his head again, and he blushed.

"Ah-ha!" she cried victoriously. Jesus, a twin sister knew you, didn't she?

They looked at each other.

"Help me and I'll talk," he said. "But I don't know that there is anything to talk about."

Daphne got close. "*Did* you get laid?"

He rolled his eyes. "I told you that. *No*."

"Tell me *some*thing!" She tossed her shoulder-length hair back.

"I met the new neighbor," he said. "He's gay."

Her eyes lit up. "Oh yeah?"

Jason almost immediately regretted telling her. He wanted to keep that fact about the mysterious man a secret. Something only he knew. But then he had to get real. This was *Daphne*. Was there anything they didn't know about each other? Sometimes *way* too much?

"Mrs. Clifford and Mrs. Livingston? Before they revolt?"

"Okay! Geez." She grabbed an order pad and headed to the sisters' table.

For a second Jason watched the coffee begin to fill its pot. Remembered Adam's coffee. He smiled. And then he turned to the refrigerator to get eggs.

ADAM had yet another piece of the quiche. A slim one this time. It really was very good. Then he eyed the coffee. Too strong, huh? What would American coffee be like? Well, he could always go over to Jason's restaurant and find out. He smiled.

Then he looked at his hat. He loved that hat. A lot. It had history behind it. A sense of dignity. Men in Monterosia wore it with great pride. What was wrong with it?

Jason had looked at it funny. Timothy Jeske—he kept thinking of the man either by his full name or as Timothy by Demand—certainly hadn't liked it. Suggested he get a baseball hat. And that thought reminded him of tonight's impending game.

He could always tell the man no. But he also wanted the work on this house done well.

Oddio!

Well, hopefully Jason would come as well and help deflect Timothy by Demand's demands.

The thought of Jason made him smile. Jason. A hero's name. Evander was said to be the man who brought the Greek pantheon of gods to Italy. Surely that was who he was named after. Unless the unlikely name of Evander was common in the United States. From the immense amount of American TV programming he'd seen, though, he couldn't recall a single character with such a name. With his love of mythology, he was sure he'd remember.

Wait a minute, he thought. Daphne. His sister. Another name from myth. A coincidence? Or a parent who loved the ancient stories?

He would love to find out.

"Yo! I been knocking on your door, man."

The sudden cry made Adam jump, and he let out a shout of his own. "*Santo cielo!*" He spun around and saw Timothy Jeske—*Timothy*—standing on the other side of the little patio fence. "*Merda!* Don't do that. You startled me." He took a deep breath. Calmed his heart. From the look on the man's face, he seemed to have startled him almost as much as Timothy had startled him.

"Sorry, dude. Didn't mean to scare you. I was just wanting you to let me in so I could start work."

Adam nodded and told him he would meet him on the porch. He picked up the quiche and placed it in the refrigerator on his way to the door, reminding himself to cover it so it wouldn't dry out. He let Timothy in and stood back while he put an armload of stuff down, including a big heavy saw and a hammer, and began to carefully inspect the floor. "You know I am going to have to rip this carpet up and throw it away, right?"

"Sì," Adam said. "Yes. I know."

"You can save some of it. Maybe use it out on your patio."

Adam nodded absently. "Maybe."

He walked over to the bookcase and gave it a little push. It was light and would be easily moved. Then he noticed the books again. *Rubyfruit Jungle*. By someone named Rita Mae Brown. He read the back cover. *Hmm….* It was about a lesbian. The cover blurb claimed the book was a "rare work of fiction that has changed real life." He might give it a go. Then he looked at the second book, an oversized paperback. *Down from Olympus*. By Jason Brewster.

He turned it over to read the back and froze less than a sentence into it.

Jason Brewster.

Wait. What?

It couldn't be.

But then of course it could, couldn't it? If this book was by the same Jason he'd met today, wouldn't it make sense that his neighbor might have had a copy of it? Adam opened the cover without reading the back. Turned to the title page. There under the title and author's name was an autograph.

> To Kathy and Melissa,
> Love you both forever,
> Jason

Kathy and Melissa. Another *hmm….* A lesbian couple? That also made sense, considering the other book. And if a lesbian couple had lived here and a gay man had lived across the alley, wouldn't they become friends? Why not? It went back to that whole idea he'd shared with Jason. The world was filled with the good and the bad. And as he'd found out his neighbor was gay, Jason might have discovered the couple who lived here were gay as well. That they were lesbians. And that was good. Someone who could understand.

For some reason his throat caught then, and for a second, he held his breath.

He thought of home and the land that he loved. But he knew he would always be alone there. He would marry some woman who could give him a child and heir. And he wouldn't love her. Not the way he should. Then he would either be terribly lonely for the rest of his life, or he'd do what so many aristocrats and noblemen and kings and presidents and prime ministers had done for as long as there were such things. He would keep a mistress… except of course his lover would be a *mantenuto*. A kept man. And it would be a secret life, with stolen moments here and there. Perhaps a week in hiding now and again.

Adam even thought his father was hinting about it to him just recently. He'd brought up the United Kingdom's Prince Charles and his marriage to Princess Diana, then spoke of his love for Camilla Bowles, the Duchess of Cornwall. How Prince Charles had wed for country and had Camilla for his heart. That the world wasn't always bleak.

Oh, and the way Father had looked at him. Adam hadn't known what to say. Or even if he was supposed to say anything. Was he hinting that if Adam would only marry as needed, he could still have a secret love?

And if the secret got out? He hadn't reminded Father how many British hated Camilla, especially for how much Charles's love of her had hurt Diana. What would the people think if Prince Amadeo Montefalcone married and had children and it came out that he didn't love his wife, but a man—

(like Jason)

—instead? Found tapes or letters or pictures that showed that love?

Would he become hated?

It was all too much to bear and the reason he'd run away. Because here he had a chance. Right?

Adam looked back down at the book in his hands. He turned it over.

> Stanley Reece is a lonely high school student, despite the fact that he is very popular and every girl wants to date him. He is lonely because he doesn't like girls. Not in the way they like him. And in his tiny town, there is just no way he can come out. Then one day he makes a crazy decision. He takes the money his grandmother had left him and books a ticket to the Greek island of Santorini for the summer.

> He has not been there one day when he catches the eye of Dominic Bourcard, an older, sophisticated, and ever-so-sexy man. Dominic is more than attracted to Stanley. He is all but enthralled. Stanley is the most beautiful young man he's ever seen. Or is he? Dominic begins to have dreams, dreams of another young man who once won his heart. And when this young man left him…. Well, he cannot remember.

> But as Stanley and Dominic begin to discover each other, they begin to share dreams. Dreams of a great eagle sweeping

down from Olympus. Claiming a young man who bears a striking resemblance to Stanley. Could it be that there is more between these two men than either ever knew or thought possible? And that it might just be time to claim one of the greatest loves of all time before it is forever too late?

God.

"Mister!"

Adam jumped, and of course it was Timothy by Demand—Timothy. He needed to start thinking of him as Timothy or he'd forget and say something stupid. Apparently Adam had gone off to Neverland again, and the handyman had been trying to ask him something.

"Sorry," he said.

"I was just asking if you could move." Timothy eyed him. "I want to get this carpet up."

"Of course. *Umm…* I have a quick errand I need to run anyway. You have my number."

And then without allowing himself to think about what he was doing, he went out the back door, out the back gate, and headed to Jason Brewster's house.

Chapter Six

JASON told his sister most of what she wanted to know when there was a lull in customers.

"Handsome?" she asked again. "Like, *guh*, handsome? Or like—" She wobbled her hand in the air. "—so-so handsome?"

He laughed. "*Really* handsome!"

"Tom Hardy handsome or Channing Tatum handsome."

"More like Ian Harding handsome... but not."

"Oh yummy!" she exclaimed, eyes flashing. Even though her boyfriend Tom was much closer to Chase Rice handsome.

"Slim, wide shoulders, brown hair that sort of falls over his forehead in the sexiest way, incredible blue eyes. Wonderful smile. *Perfect* teeth." He had a thing about teeth. Too crooked or one missing ruined it for him for some reason. Daphne was nodding. She knew all about that. "Maybe thirty years old," he continued. "And maybe three or four inches taller than me."

Now her eyes went huge. "Uh-oh!"

"What?" he asked.

"Your dreams of having to lift your head just a little bit when you kiss…."

He grinned and blushed for the hundredth time that day. Nodded.

"And he's gay? For sure? Your gaydar isn't all that great."

Which was true. He'd gotten crushes here or there on the worst possible men. Men who might punch a gay boy. She'd had to rescue him once.

"He told me he's gay."

"Well that's a plus." She sipped her coffee from a mug that said John Deere. Almost none of the mugs at the Patch matched. He thought it was part of the charm. "When do I meet him?"

"Daphne! Give me a day or five, okay?" He laughed again. "Criminy!" Because, God, an overprotective sister could ruin everything.

She looked at him knowingly. "You think I'll scare him off, don't you?"

He gave her a slight shrug. What could he say?

She put hands on hips. "I have never scared a guy away that you were interested in."

Jason raised an eyebrow, thinking of a dark-haired lovely who lived two blocks down and had always made his heart pitter-patter.

"Who?" she asked, almost glowering.

"You know who," he said, because how many gay men were there in Buckman? In that moment, he could smell him and the colognes he liked to wear.

"Oh. *Him*." Daphne shook her head. "That's because he was totally *not* right for you. And I didn't scare him off. I just sat down with him one day because he'd been walking around with this hangdog expression and asked him what was wrong."

Jason knew the story. Daphne had told him how the guy had fallen in love with this best friend and messed everything up, and the best friend had moved away.

"I *had* to tell him to get the hell of out Buckman and go get him!"

"Yeah, yeah," Jason said, and waved the comment away. "Whatever. The point is that he was gay, and there aren't any gay men in this town."

Daphne laughed. "Of course there are. They say 10 percent, right? That means there's a shitload of them. They're just more discreet, and if you can't get your gaydar to work, you're going to have to learn to find them another way."

He shrugged. And thought of Adam. "Well, there is a gay man in Buckman now. And if I'm lucky…."

"You *are* lucky," Daphne said. "You've made yourself a very nice life. One that doesn't revolve around Walmart or Deriddere, Inc."

Which was the other business that was the lifeblood of the town. One that didn't exploit its employees. Or at least not so much.

"The Briar Patch is your way to be you. You're making it work. And you're out, for God's sake. And no one has burned a cross in your front yard. No one spits at you. No one toilet papers your house. No one spray-paints 'faggot' on your car."

He nodded absently. Yeah. He guessed it was true. And he loved the Patch.

But he stilled dreamed of eagles….

"Be you," Daphne advised. "And make sure he isn't a jerk. If he's a good guy, how will he be able to resist you?"

He smiled weakly. "Thanks, Daphne."

"If not the new guy, someone will finally have the balls to admit he's gay and walk through that door."

"You think?"

The bell over the front door tinkled. They both turned casually to see who it was.

Jason barely stifled a gasp.

Daphne didn't repress one.

It was Adam Terranova.

A LITTLE bell jingled as Adam opened the door to The Briar Patch. What he saw inside was delightful. It was a room as wide as his house and as long, but open. He stood among chest-high bookshelves stuffed to overflowing. Hardcovers, paperbacks, oversized books. Oh, what joy! What treasures were just waiting to be found? Right there in front of him was a thick volume with the complete tales of Sherlock Holmes!

But then he saw Jason.

Bellissimo!

Jason flashed his lovely smile Adam's way, and it was hard to believe he was real. There was a girl at his side—a young woman actually—who resembled him. She was openly staring. He blushed. "*Buongiorno,*" he said, and throwing caution to the wind once more, took off his sunglasses.

The girl. She was all but gaping at him!

"Adam," Jason said. "You came."

"Jesus H. Christ!" the girl said, jerking her head in Jason's direction. "*That's* him?"

"Daphne!" Jason snapped, eyes wide.

Allora! The sister.

He stepped up to the counter behind which they stood. Beyond them he could see a kitchen with a gas-burning stove, a couple of microwaves, a refrigerator, and a small table covered in flour. He didn't miss Jason elbowing his sister in the ribs, though, and his sharp hearing caught the "Stop staring!"

"Sì, Jason. I came. To get out of Mr. Jeske's way—"

"Jeske?" Daphne hissed. "*Timmy* Jeske?"

Another elbow.

She really was lovely. She reminded him of bit of the singer Katy Perry. Lovely. But not as beautiful as Jason. Adam looked at her. "You must be the sister he had such kind words about."

Her eyes went wide. So yes. It was a family thing. He smiled.

Daphne looked at her brother. "You had kind words to say about me?"

Jason flashed him a look, and Adam gave him a wink.

"Always," Jason said.

Now *she* was blushing.

"So, you're the new neighbor. Jason has had a few kind things to say about you too."

He turned his ambassador smile on her, and when she reached out a hand—to shake, perhaps?—he took it, bent at the waist, and kissed it. "*Incantato,*" he said.

She giggled. "You have permission to date my brother!" she blurted.

"Daphne!" Jason cried, obviously aggrieved. Which hurt just a bit. Because did that mean Jason hadn't liked what she said.

She gave her brother an are-you-kidding-me look and said, "Well he *does*!"

Jason was bright red now and turned to Adam. "I'm sorry. She just blurts stuff out."

Daphne turned to Adam as well. "I call 'em like I see 'em."

"Perhaps your brother doesn't *want* to date me," he said, hoping otherwise.

"Oh, he—"

Another elbow to her side. Strong enough to make her curse. "Really, Jason?"

"Really, Daphne. Remember what I said?"

"You said a lot of things," she snapped.

"And now I'm asking you to amscray, okay?"

Amscray? Now what could that possibly mean?

"Yeah, yeah." She rolled her eyes. "I just remembered I have a very important errand I have to do," she said. Then she held out her hand, palm down, knuckles up. "It was a pleasure to meet you. I hope we get to talk soon."

"That would be delizioso," he said, turning on all his charm. Because sometimes when you won over a family member, the door was open for you to enter the house.

"Delich-e-so to you too," she said, mangling the word but with a charm of her own. At least she had figured out what it meant. Sometimes the English word didn't leap to his tongue. She looked back at Jason as she made her way to the front door. "Maybe I'll come back for the lunch rush?" she asked over a shoulder.

"*Please*, Daphne?" Of course with his eyes wide.

"*If* I get my errand done!" And she was out the door.

And they were alone.

Chapter Seven

"PLEASE forgive my sister," Jason said, wishing he could read this whole situation. The problem, though, was he lacked experience. He was twenty-five, and except for his secret "affair" with Tim, he'd never done anything like dating or courting. Sure, he'd seen dozens of chick flicks. Seen the heroes charm the heroines. Seen Leonardo DiCaprio get through Kate Winslet's icy exterior so that she was soon asking him to "draw me like one of your French girls." But how did he do that? Or know if it was being done to him?

He didn't know how to play the love game.

Hell! He didn't even know how to play the sex game!

"There is nothing to forgive," Adam said. Of course he did. He was European. A gentleman first and forever.

"She is all about open mouth, insert foot," Jason said.

"Stick... foot in... the mouth? Do I understand?" Adam asked.

Jason laughed. "It means saying the worst thing you could and not realizing you've said such a dumb thing. Sometimes it can mean you open your mouth and stuff falls out, and you don't think about the consequences of what you are saying."

Adam shook his head. "I don't know how the foot gets to be a part of it. We have something we say. *Parlare solo perché si ha la lingua in bocca.* To speak only because you have a tongue in your mouth. It means the same thing, I think. To say something simply because you can."

"Yeah," Jason said. He thought about it. "That is better. It certainly sounds like my sister."

"What I mean to say," Adam continued, "is don't let it bother you at all. I like her. Your sister. She is funny. Charming."

Daphne? Charming. Jason laughed. Decided to go with it. "She is what she is."

Adam nodded. "Bread for bread and wine for wine."

Jason didn't even ask.

Adam stepped closer to the counter.

God. Jason swallowed hard. *I'm twelve*, he thought. And giggling with the other girls about the new boy in class. *Get a hold of yourself! You're being stupid! You just met him! Love doesn't just walk into a bookstore!*

"I hope you don't mind, but—"

But what? Jason wondered.

"—I found this in my house." And he held up Jason's book.

Down from Olympus. His *first* book.

It surprised the heck out of him.

"This is you, no?"

God, that voice. Like windchimes. Like poetry. Was he trying to sound that darned sexy?

"It's... it's me," he said. Found he was embarrassed and didn't know why. The cover was sexy, with two shirtless men, one standing taller than the other, looking into each other's eyes. But it wasn't porn. Why should he be embarrassed? He was proud of it. He'd poured his heart and soul into it. And it wasn't like a book about two men falling in love should shock Adam!

"You wrote this?" Adam asked, and was that a look of wonder on his face?

Jason nodded. "Yes."

"*Forte.* How wonderful. Why didn't you tell me you were a writer?"

And Jason could see he really was excited. Now *that* was wonderful.

"We didn't have that much time."

"True," Adam agreed. "Allora. I am sure there are all kinds of things I don't know about you."

He stepped closer again, and that was it. Jason's heart was pretty much in his throat.

Yes. Adam was a little taller than him. So that Jason would have to tilt his head back just a bit for them to kiss.

God! *Get a hold of yourself!*

"I... I don't know. I don't think there's that much to tell."

Adam shook his head. "I don't think so. I think there is probably much to tell." He held up the book. "I read the back cover. About your heroes. Falling in love. And an eagle. Is the eagle Zeus, perhaps?"

Jason's mouth fell open. He closed it. "Yes. You knew?"

Adam moved in so that he was right against the counter between them. "I come from near where the eagle flew." He wet his lips.

Kiss me!

The bell over the front door rang.

"Goddammit!" he cried.

And then looked right into the shocked face of his mother.

THE woman looked to be maybe in her fifties, with very large hazel eyes with lines just beginning at their corners, long, high, exquisite cheekbones, and shoulder-length brown hair only starting to silver. If it wasn't for the bright sunlight pouring in through the window in the door, Adam didn't think he would have noticed.

"Jason! I thought I raised you better than that!"

Ah. Now the mother. Even with the difference in coloring, he should have seen it in her eyes.

A family affair now.

"Mom, what are you doing here?" Jason asked.

"What? I'm not welcome?" she asked.

"Of course you are." He smiled at her. At Adam. "You're always welcome. It's just you *never* come by."

She was looking at Adam now, though, and not her son. She was wearing a blue women's dress suit and carrying a rather large bag, also blue. She tilted her head, narrowed her eyes slightly. "Hello," she said.

Adam bobbed his head slightly, not quite a bow. The way his mother taught him that a prince would show respect, but remember that he was in fact a prince. Was she a signora or a signorina? Could he assume? He decided to. "Signora," he replied.

"Mom," Jason said. "This is Adam."

She glanced at her son then returned her gaze to him. The moment seemed to last forever. He wished he was wearing his sunglasses. And his hat. But maybe not.

That might have been worse. Then, "Well, since my son isn't going to introduce me—"

"*Mom!*"

It was only then Adam saw the slight raise of one of her brows and a smile teasing one corner of her mouth. "I'm Iris Brewster." She held out a hand.

He decided not to kiss it, but shook it instead.

"Adam's moved here recently from Italy," Jason said. "He bought the house behind me." He cocked a thumb over his shoulder.

"Italy? I've always wanted to go. It's at the very top of my bucket list."

"You should go, signora. It is a country for beautiful women." Hoping that was the right approach.

She spared another glance at Jason. "A charmer, eh?" she asked.

Jason blushed, and her eyes narrowed again. She shifted more in his direction.

"Yes, Mom."

Adam decided on a different approach. "Iris. She was the goddess of the rainbow."

Finally, a real smile! Her eyes widened slightly, and now he knew where the quirk in the Brewster children came from.

She nodded. "Yes," she said.

"Were you named for her, or is Iris a family name? Or maybe your mother loves the flower?"

Her raised eyebrow settled. "The goddess," she said. "Do you know how few times I've been asked that?"

"One look should tell them you are a special woman." It was a risk.

Now the brow rose again "Oh, you are the one, aren't you?"

"The one?" he asked, not quite sure what she meant.

"You know what to say. I'd guess in just about any situation."

His face warmed. He had been trained. This was a sharp woman.

"Iris was also the messenger of the gods," he said instead of answering her. "And the goddesses of the sea and the sky."

Another glance at her son.

"Mother also loved the flowers," she said then, apparently instead of responding to his distraction. "She had a beautiful collection. We moved most of them to our house—my husband's and mine—when we found out the people who bought her place were going to get rid of them in favor of a lawn."

"*Ridicolo!*" he declared.

"Indeed," she said with a nod. "Jason has some of them out back. A few out front as well. You should check them out."

"I will."

She gave him one last long look and then turned back to her son. "I was taking care of some legal things for the library today, Jason. Thought I'd stop by and remind you of this Saturday."

Ah. She worked for the library. More books. He loved it.

"I didn't forget, Mother," Jason said with a roll of his eyes.

"Well good. I didn't think you would. Your sister maybe. But not you."

"Daphne won't forget."

She nodded.

"What kind of quiche did you make today? Any left?"

"I've got a couple pieces of the pear and Roquefort cheese."

"Of course you do," she said with a sigh.

"You don't like it?" Adam asked.

"I love it! It's amazing. But most of the people of our fair city have rather plebian tastes, so he doesn't make it that often."

"Would you like a piece, Mom?" Jason asked.

"I'd like you to package me up one." She gave Adam another look, and now her eyes were flashing like her daughter's. "Italy, you say? Where?"

"Ro—" He started to say Rome, as his manufactured autobiography said. But for some reason he didn't want to lie to her.

He certainly couldn't tell her he was the prince of Monterosia, though, could he? He thought it might be a mistake to even mention his country. This was a keen mind here. Not one to be trifled with.

"I've spent a lot of time in Rome," he said. "But lately I've been living near Trieste." Which wasn't a lie. The palace was twenty-five kilometers or so from there, but considering how far Rome was, Trieste *was* close. Now he only had to remember to tell his brother so they kept everything straight.

"I'm not sure I've heard of Trieste," she said. "I'll have to look it up."

Look it up? I'm getting more and more in trouble.

Jason stepped between them. "Here, Mom," he said, handing her a small brown paper bag with the words The Briar Patch stamped on the side. "Two pieces."

She smiled. "Thank you, baby. It will be a wonderful lunch. I may even let your father have a piece."

"Wow! That would be different." Jason put a hand on his hip.

Her eyes grew distant for a moment, and that half smile formed on her face again. "He's been... a good boy lately." Then she was back. Eyes flashing. Another characteristic of the Brewsters?

"Mom!" Was that real or mock shock on his face.

She looked to the ceiling with a partial roll of her eyes. "I'm sixty-four, Jason. Not a hundred and sixty-four."

"Ma dai…." The words were out of Adam's mouth before he could stop them. Sixty-four? This woman was sixty-four?

He saw they were both staring at him.

"I think perhaps you have a painting in your attic," he said, gazing at Iris.

"I think perhaps you're full of—"

"Mom!" Jason cried again.

"That or you're trying to get in my son's pants."

Now it was Adam's turn for his eyes to go wide.

"Mom!" Jason looked horrified. Adam *was* horrified.

She turned to Jason. "Mom! Mom! Mom! You sound like those seagulls in *Finding Nemo*. I should know. I had to watch it nine million times when you and your sister were little."

"But M—"

She held up a hand. "Don't say it." Her head swiveled in Adam's direction. Pointed at him. "Be nice to my son. He's a sweetheart. And he's lonely. Hurt him and know my wrath. After all, I'm the messenger of the gods. You don't know who I'll go to."

Jason rolled his eyes dramatically, and Adam burst into laughter, felt his cheeks grow hot.

"I mean it. Rhamnusia perhaps. Or Adrestia."

"Handmaiden of Nemesis," Adam replied. "Goddess of retribution."

"And sublime balance between good and evil. Are you good or evil, Adam?"

"I like to think of myself as good," he said with a slight bow.

She eyed him one more time. "Maybe I'll see you Saturday?"

"It's not just for family?" he asked. Because that is what it had sounded like.

"And friends of family."

"I think I might like to be a friend of the family," he said.

She nodded. "You'd be wise."

The she leaned in to her son and kissed his cheek and told him to "Be careful. Be safe." And to Adam, "*Be safe*," over Jason's indignant cries, and "Make him show you the irises." With that she left.

Her departure left a huge hole in the room.

Finally Jason said, "I'm sorry about my mother."

"No need," Adam replied. "I like her." He did. She was formidable. And for a bit there, he'd thought that was something he wouldn't find in Buckman, Missouri.

And he thought he liked Jason too. He just wasn't sure what word he would pick for him yet. Besides bellissimo, that was.

Then, once again, the bell over the door rang, and when he looked, who should it be but Timothy, his new handyman?

"Sorry to bother you, Adam." He spared a funny look at Jason. "But I have some questions for you before I can go on. Can you come look?"

Adam sighed inwardly. "Sure," he said. "Of course." He turned back to Jason. "I must go."

"You didn't pick out a book," Jason said.

Adam glanced around him, saw the book on Sherlock Holmes, and pulled it off the shelf. "This one," he said and placed it on the counter, reached for his wallet.

"Take it as a housewarming present," Jason said, smiling his brightest yet.

"No. I mustn't. You have a business to run, and I've read that is not always easy in a small town. I insist."

Jason half shrugged. He opened the book, saw the price, and rang it up on his little ancient register. Then he helped Adam with the correct amount of cash. Their fingers touched. It was electric. Just that little bit.

"Look!" said Timothy. "I'll see you at the house?"

"Be there in one minute," he said without looking.

The screen door closed with a bang Adam hardly noticed.

"Please?" he asked. "You come over for the baseball game tonight? I'll fix us dinner."

Jason's face lit up. He nodded. "Sure."

"I look forward to it, then," Adam said and left the place a minute later, feeling better than he had since he'd made the decision to leave home.

Chapter Eight

NERVOUS was not the word for what Jason was that evening.

He was going over to Adam's house.

A gorgeous, mysterious *gay* man. A man who, as far as he could tell, was interested in him. He hadn't had a man interested in him since Timmy.

Who was also going to be at Adam's place. With a six-pack.

Groan.

For a second he saw Timmy naked. Saw him doing all kinds of wonderful things. Oh, the things that so-called straight man did with his mouth and how blazingly sexy it had been looking down at him while he did it. But that was the past. Before Timmy called him a faggot. Before he got engaged. Had he told Adam that he was engaged? Would Adam care? Just because the beautiful Italian man was classy didn't mean he wanted anything more than sex. And hadn't he heard that men from Italy were lovers? Lovers of lots of people?

So maybe Adam wouldn't care that Tim was getting married. Maybe he'd sleep with him anyway. The thought made Jason stop halfway across his backyard, carrying a small Crock-Pot with cheese dip and a bag of tortilla chips.

No. Adam didn't want to sleep with Tim. Wasn't that the reason Adam had invited him over?

He started walking again and then stopped once more, right in the middle of the gravel alley.

So the only reason he was invited was so that Adam wouldn't have to have sex with Tim? *He'd do it anyway if I weren't there?*

You're overthinking this. You're nervous.

Of course I'm nervous!

Because he thought sleeping with Adam could be a very wonderful thing.

He closed his eyes. Saw the man's lovely eyes and perfect skin and flashing white teeth and heard his laughter. Wondered. Wondered what he would look like without that shirt. It hadn't hid much. His pants hadn't either. Oh, what would he look like naked?

There was a stirring in the crotch of Jason's pants, and if he didn't want what was between his legs pointing his way into Adam's house, he knew he'd better think of something else.

He started walking again. The Crock-Pot was getting heavy.

What if Tim was already there? What if he was doing things to Adam with his mouth?

That thought took care of his erection.

He went right to the little fence around the patio—the piazza—and reached over and placed the standard baseball-fame snack on the little table where he and Adam had eaten quiche this morning. Funny how something so small could get so heavy. But then it was a full log of Velveeta cheese and a can of diced tomatoes and green chilies. Not bowling ball heavy of course, but holding it out ahead of him so that it didn't mess up his white pants while he was daydreaming didn't make for a light load either.

White pants! What in the hell made him pick white pants?

Because they were tight, and Daphne said they made his butt look good.

"Really good," she'd said. "If you weren't my brother...." And she'd patted him right on the rear.

"Eeewww!" he cried, and they'd both laughed.

I wore these to look hot for Adam.

But what if he only wanted pleasure?

Then I'll go for it, dammit. I haven't had sex in seven years!

There had been a chance or two.

A bathroom in a rest area.

Clyde Hanley, a coworker back in his days at Deriddere, manufacturers of the "world-famous" Roll & Step, the very rolling stepstool his mother had once fallen from. Over weeks it had happened. A slow building friendship, then doing things after work. Knees touching when they went to movies, leaning into each other a time or two when they'd had a few too many beers at Duck Inn Bottoms. Then the first kiss on the back porch of Clyde's house—and being caught by overly religious parents. The screaming had been epic. And even though Clyde had been over twenty-one, the religion had won out, and he'd quit Deriddere, Inc. and moved to California to live with his sister. Jason never heard from him again.

Then there was a guy he'd met at Buckman's annual Summer Fun Days. Playing the game where you throw the Ping-Pong ball and try and get it in the little bowls with goldfish in them. It was the whole eye-thing he'd read about countless times on the internet. First from a hundred feet away. The glance. The second look. Eyes locking. The weaving dance through the crowds of people. The pretending not to look at each other as they threw Ping-Pong balls that were almost impossible to get in the tiny goldfish bowls without hitting the edge and bouncing away.

Except the guy—he had gorgeous curly blond hair and dark eyes and tattoos on big arms revealed by a tank top—did win. And asked Jason if he wanted the goldfish. Romantic. Sweet. They wound up in the guy's car, and they made out, and it was so incredible, and they'd steamed up the windows.

And then, of course, Jason's mother had called. Dad had had a wee too much to drink, and she had a cast on her foot from when she'd fallen off a stepstool at the library and broken her ankle. They needed a ride home.

Jason and the guy had exchanged phone numbers and texted each other until late, and the man invited him to his place the next town over. Twenty minutes.

And in that time Jason had chickened out.

He didn't want to be just a fuck.

So, what's the difference now?

Seven years. That was the difference.

And if sex was all Adam wanted? It was touch. It was being held. He knew it would mean being kissed.

Which was something he needed very much.

ADAM was more than relieved when he heard Jason call out through the back door. He had made it before Timothy. That was what Adam had hoped for.

But it was more than that, and as he went to greet Jason, he couldn't help but smile.

Bellissimo, he thought to himself.

"*Una bellezza mozzafiato*," he said aloud. The words came unbidden. Breathtaking. That was what Jason was, standing there looking at him. He'd opened the gate, and there Jason stood, seeming to glow in the evening sunlight. Those eyes! So blue. Like the Mediterranean. The sun shone off his dark hair. He was wearing a plaid blue-and-white button-down shirt that was tucked into white pants that showed Adam he was right. Jason had a delicious body. Lean, but not too skinny.

He wanted to take him into his arms and kiss him at that very moment.

"What?" Jason asked, breaking the spell. At least temporarily.

Adam's cheeks heated ever so slightly. "Perhaps I will tell you later."

Jason smiled and oh, bello, so lovely….

Calm yourself. He's the first gay man you've met.

Well, besides Timothy.

But the first who had made him feel like this.

Hormones!

And the fact that I haven't been with a man in so long. Especially one that hadn't made him feel a bit ashamed afterward. Dangerous liaisons that could have hurt him and his family and country. Fumblings in dark alleys. One or the other dropping to their knees with no preamble. No emotion. Certainly no kiss. Only lust.

Only pent-up desire and release. Leaving him feeling more alone than he'd felt before.

And of course, none of this had happened at home. Only on his trips to Italy.

What if he had been hurt? Truly hurt? Killed even? What would that have done to his home and family and people?

That was the real reason for his shame.

"Are you all right?" Jason asked, stepping onto the piazza. Or what Adam had decided this little patio with its red-and-gray cement paving stones was. Was to him.

He nodded. "I am fine."

"You seemed to go away there for a second. You looked sad."

Jason was perceptive. Gods....

"Sorry. Please, please. Prego. Welcome." He saw the Crock-Pot then. "You brought something? I said I would feed us."

"Ah...." Jason shrugged. "It's just Ro-Tel cheese dip. Sort of a tradition when dudes are sitting around watching sports."

Adam stepped closer. "I have not heard of this hotel cheese dip. It is good? No?"

Jason burst into laughter. "Ro-Tel dip," he said. "And yes. It's very good, although not probably so good for you."

He opened the lid to give Adam a peek. The cheese was orange instead of pale, like mozzarella. It smelled wonderful. "But pleasurable. Something to indulge in."

A funny look flashed across Jason's face but was gone as quickly as it came. Nothing, probably. Nerves.

"Y-yes. We Americans always feel guilty about pursuing pleasures."

"That is too bad. We should love life's pleasures. Take them while we can."

That look again.

Adam took a breath. "You don't agree?"

Jason gave a half shrug.

"But I understand, though. The guilt sometimes. Because I am a—" He froze, surprised at what he'd almost said. "Because I have duties," he quickly amended. "There are many things that most people can indulge in that I cannot."

He couldn't have spoken more truth.

"Or at least rarely," he said softly, and he imagined what Jason's lips would feel like against his own.

But the comment seemed to brush away any "funny" expressions Jason may have worn. He was smiling again. At least a bit. Adam loved it when Jason smiled.

"Where do you want it?" Jason asked, moving to pick up the pot with the glass lid. And look. There was an electric cord sticking from it!

"Here, let me take that," Adam said. "You get the door?"

"Sure," Jason said, and turned, went to it, opened it, held it open, and gave Adam a glimpse of one the prettiest bottoms he'd ever seen.

He gulped. "Go, please, on in. I will catch it."

Adam got the screen door with his elbow before it could swing closed and got a better look at Jason's bottom as well. It was praiseworthy in those tight white pants. One to do Michelangelo proud.

"Something smells good," Jason said walking down the narrow length of the kitchen.

"I am making your American hot dogs," he said as he placed the pot of cheese on the counter next to the small stove. "I wasn't sure how to cook them."

Cook would have been stunned at how small the kitchen was, the *stove* was. Adam figured the whole thing could have gone in one of the ovens in the huge palace kitchen. Adam's house would have fit in the kitchen. The first floor of Jason's home would have fit. Both houses combined would have made it with room to spare.

But then the palace kitchen wouldn't have made for such intimate quarters. There was barely room to open the oven door and show Jason the hot dogs laid out neatly on a cookie sheet. He closed the door and noticed that if he leaned up against the green counter— like he was doing now—Jason would have to turn to his side to inch past him. The front of Jason's pants would probably brush against his ass, wouldn't it?

Adam shivered.

He turned around. And if he leaned back against the counter—like he was doing now—Jason would have to do the same thing. Inch past him. But this time their crotches might touch.

Adam's cock began to stir.

If he didn't stop these kinds of thoughts, that brushing would almost certainly happen, wouldn't it?

His throat went dry, and he swallowed. His nostrils flared. Was that Jason's scent. A slight masculine musk. Maybe the tiniest hint of sweet? His eyes widened as he took Jason in. Those eyes, those lips he so wanted to kiss, that long throat.

Jason was looking back. Adam saw Jason's Adam's apple bob as *he* swallowed.

He wants this….

Or does he?

Dammit, but he had so little experience. The possibilities of the dance… the flirting… with a man… in the light of the sun. Even the late-evening sun.

"Jason?" he whispered, emboldened enough to ask.

"Yes?" Jason replied, his voice a sigh.

There was a knock on the front door. "Yo!" came a shout.

Another pounding knock.

Timothy.

They both sighed together. Looked into each other's eyes. For a moment Adam thought Jason might kiss him.

And then Timothy called out, "I'm coming in! Ready or not."

Adam wasn't ready.

But the bread was the bread; the wine was the wine. It was what it was.

The door opened, and in came Timothy. He was carrying two six-packs.

He was grinning too.

At the both of them.

Chapter Nine

TIMOTHY was grinning at both of them. At least that's what it looked like to Jason.

He was standing in the doorway to the kitchen wearing running shorts and a T-shirt that said KC Royal Champions 2014. He was eyeing them both. He held up the two six-packs of bottled beer. "Hey, boys. I decided to double up." He winked. "And it ain't the 3.2 shit from Wallymart either. I wanted us to have *fun*."

Jason had no doubt what Timmy really meant.

He shook his head.

This was the man who'd called him faggot at the Duck Inn Bottoms. Insane. What was going on?

"Let me take those," Adam said and did so. When he turned his back on Tim to put them in the apartment-sized refrigerator, the daggers were back in Jason's high school lover's eyes. They were aimed at Jason.

He sighed. Considered leaving. And then thought about Tim doing things to Adam with his mouth, and he just couldn't stand it. He crossed his arms and stared back. *Do your worst.*

"Do you... boys... want one now?" Adam asked, his head practically in the fridge, his ass pointed out at them both. A muscular, full ass. Jason couldn't help but stare. Could he blame Tim for doing the same?

"I sure do," growled Tim.

God. How could this be happening?

Tim had called him a faggot.

Tim was engaged.

And Tim hadn't so much as winked at him in passing since he'd gotten back from college five years ago!

He was wetting his lips.

"Me too," Jason said, catching Tim's eyes with some daggers of his own.

Adam stood and handed bottles over. "I think I have an opener here somewhere," he said, reaching for a drawer handle.

"No need," Tim said. "They're twist offs." And he demonstrated.

Adam looked surprised. "*Che forte!*"

"What?" Tim asked. "You don't have none of these wherever you come from?"

Adam shook his head and tried to open it. Hissed.

"Here, mon-*shure*," Tim said and took the bottle from him, twisted the top off with flair, and tossed it in the sink with a clatter. It was surprisingly loud.

He handed the bottle back to Adam, then raised his. "What do we drink to, boys?"

"How about to new friends?" Adam offered.

"Yes," Jason said and raised his bottle. "To new friends."

Adam eyed them both. "And old?"

"Yeah." Tim gave a nod and looked at Jason. "Sure. To old friends."

Jason nodded, and they clinked bottles.

They drank.

When they lowered their beers, there was a short silence. Adam, thank goodness, broke it.

"The hot dogs will be done soon, I think. I will need your help in the living room, though. We have a… little hole in our way to watch the game?"

"Hole?" Jason asked.

"That's one word for it," Tim said and gestured toward the living room.

Jason peeked over Tim's shoulder. Half the floor was gone!

"That was the little problem I mentioned," Adam said.

Tim stepped back, and Jason walked in to see a very narrow area with a wooden floor. The rest was dirt. Fairly hard-packed earth to be sure. But dirt. A couch stood on its end in one corner.

"I thought that maybe if we move the couch *just* into the hole," Adam said, "the three of us could sit and watch the television here." He pointed at the flat-screen against the wall. It was one of the few things waiting for him when he'd moved in. You could order almost anything online. "If we put it close enough to the flooring, we won't have to put our feet in the dirt."

It would be almost like sitting on the floor. But at least a comfortable floor.

"Fuck," Tim said. "Why the hell not?"

So that was what they did. The three of them lowered the couch onto its feet, being careful not to flip it into the hole since the living room was small before half the floor was cut away. Then between them they got it situated on the dirt floor, the front end of the couch against the wooden floor. And indeed, the seating level was almost even with it. It would be very much like sitting on the floor, but a comfortable one. With a back to lean on.

This was going to be interesting.

While Adam was in the kitchen, Tim grabbed Jason's arm. Firmly, but not enough to hurt.

"You had to be here?" he asked. His tone was odd. Like some strange mixture of anger and fear. It was in his eyes too.

"Really?" Jason wanted to ask him.

My God.

It made him feel sad. For more than one reason. That desperate look. He understood to a degree. Wasn't it a desperate need that brought him here himself? Hadn't he decided right outside the house, on the way over, that he'd forego what he longed for in his heart to just… be… touched. He couldn't judge Tim.

But Tim had also called him faggot.

And he was engaged.

What the hell was he doing here?

"I thought…," he started to say and then stopped.

I thought what? That you decided you were straight and asked a girl to marry you?

Maybe that was it?

He was engaged… but *not* married. At least not yet. Maybe he wanted one last taste of the forbidden fruit?

Tim trembled. Not something Jason thought a tough guy like him would do. There was fear here. But fear of what?

"Timmy?"

He grimaced. "*Timothy*," he snapped. "Don't call me Timmy."

Jason thought of them holding each other, covered in sweat, panting, inside a pup tent down by the creek, and wondered how he could ever think of him as Timothy.

Oh, he'd been so surprised to see Timmy yesterday. *Timothy*. Jason hadn't seen him in ages, and in a town as small as Buckman, that was unusual. *Timothy* had changed since high school. He'd been so magnificently *fit* in those days. Like one of the ancient statues Jason admired so very much. Hermes perhaps. Mercury. And now?

Well, he certainly wasn't fat. But he was… well… padded. His face seemed a little broader. He had a paunch he never would have allowed back when he did a hundred sit-ups a day. Jason knew it was that many because sometimes he kneeled on Tim's feet while he did them (sometimes that gave Jason a sexy peek up his shorts leg) and counted them off. Tim usually did that many crunches as well. But paunch or not, his arms were still huge, biceps popping even when holding up six-packs of beer. His thighs were still mighty as well. And Jason remembered those thighs. Being between them.

Was it bad to have lustful thoughts for a man who had called him such an ugly name? Because after all, Timmy had once called him much sweeter ones.

Timothy.

Who knew what was going on inside Timothy's head. Should Jason just leave now? Leave Adam to him? Jason didn't like the idea, but was that pride? His own desperation? Anger that a man who had called him faggot wanted Adam for his own? And what of this other possibility? The two six-packs. The way he'd grinned at them both. Winked. Used words like "double up" and "I wanted us to have fun." Surely that was sexual innuendo if there ever was. He was suggesting a three-way, Jason was sure. Could he do that? Could he be with his old lover that way again? With the man Jason wanted so much today? Did the idea of climbing into bed with the two of them excite or disgust him?

He didn't know. Maybe it did both!

Then Adam was standing at the kitchen threshold, letting them know they could have the hot dogs—he loved the way Adam pronounced "haut doegs"— anytime they wanted.

"Let's find the game first," Jason said. "You can turn the oven to warm so they don't get cold."

Adam allowed that sounded fine, and luckily he'd already had cable turned on. In no time at all, they found the right channel.

JASON and Timothy loaded up their plates, and Adam was grateful that he seemed to have done everything right. It was a simple meal, but sometimes the simplest things were the easiest to mess up. Luckily, he'd found a woman pushing a shopping cart and apparently preparing for the game as well. There were so many varieties of hot dogs, he hadn't known where to begin. Or if anything went with them.

"Get the all-beef kind," she'd said. She was a big woman, with a pink sheer scarf covering hair curlers the size of soda pop cans, wearing multicolored stretch pants and a T-shirt that declared Go Buckman Badgers—which it seemed was the local high school sports team. He had seen the head of an animal that might have been a badger on the Buckman water tower and wondered what it was. Now he knew.

"Those other dogs," the woman said, pointing at the dozen or more brands of hot dogs as if they were offensive, "have all kinds of shit in 'em. Stomachs an' intestines, pig snouts and worms and eyeballs and mouse turds and even cock-ah-roaches. I have a cousin who was married to a woman whose mother's sister found a pull tab in one ah her's once."

Adam wasn't sure what a pull tab was, but he told her he thought he'd "like the kind without those *or* mouse… droppings."

"Well, listen to you, all elegant and stuff." Then she picked up a package and thrust it toward him. "See? *All* beef with no fillers. That means they ain't got no worms or shit. Me and my husband *loves* 'em! Not only is they nice and fat, which means you get more bang for your buck but you don't have to worry about bitin' into one and then see it lookin' back atcha."

Adam hadn't known whether to laugh or be disgusted.

"How many should I get?" he asked.

"How many ah yahs is gonna be eatin' 'em?"

"Well, I think three," he replied. "Three men. About my age."

"Well, my husband"—she reached behind her and pulled at her spandex—"can eat about a hunnert of 'em. He's a big man, though. Lookin' at you…?" She eyed him up and down. "I'd say no more'n four at the upmost. Them other boys about your size?"

He nodded. "Yes, signora."

Her eyebrows shot up so high they nearly disappeared under her scarf. She cleared her throat. "You ain't from around here, are you?" she asked.

He shook his head and was glad for his sunglasses. "Rome." He almost said "France" as well, but stopped himself at the last second.

The woman advised him how many hot dogs to buy for three men and also explained about buns and… fixins'?

"You'll be wanting some ketchup and some mustard—get the kind that comes from France and not that nasty poop-on kind. Get some relish too. Don't forget the buns. Oh! Some people like sauerkraut too. You might think about getting you a can."

His spine stiffened at that. *No* sauerkraut. Not for any reason. It was a matter of pride. When Austria took over the region of Italy directly next to Monterosia, they highly influenced the people there, even though they insisted they were still Italians. Sauerkraut, by the bucket it seemed, was one of those influences. Monterosia had managed to keep their freedom during that time and others in history, if sometimes only by a hair's breadth. Or as his people would say, *per il rotto della cuffia*, "to escape despite your broken helmet." The palace, a fortress more than anything, helped. Even after all these years, they refused to allow the dish past their borders, let alone in their kitchen or on their dinner tables.

Thankfully, no one commented, or even seemed to notice its absence. They got their hot dogs and dressed them how they wanted—Timothy put some of the Ro-Tel sauce right on his.

And there were chips too.

"Don't get the Lay's," the woman had told him. "They ain't no better than the Great Value brand, and they're twice as much."

No one seemed to care he'd bought the cheaper brand.

No. Instead they got their food and gathered in the living room (Timothy insisted on dividing them and sitting in the middle of the couch), and they stuffed themselves and proceeded to watch Adam's first baseball game ever.

Chapter Ten

ADAM discovered he liked baseball. At first it was confusing. It seemed to have far more rules than necessary—many of them contradictory. But by the sixth inning, he had it pretty well understood, even the scoring symbols on the television screen. He felt the rush, the thrill, and found himself cheering and leaning in and bouncing in his seat.

Almost engaged enough to be able to ignore the way Timothy's leg was pressing into his.

Almost enough to be tempted to press back.

But then he would look over at the beauty that was Jason in profile, eyes wide with excitement. Or sometimes he would catch Jason looking back at him. Adam's breath would catch, or he'd forget to breathe at all. *Bellisimo!* He was like a flawless statue come to life.

Yes, Adam knew that Timothy wanted him. But if he read Jason correctly, so did Jason.

And who would he rather have? There was really no choice.

So when Timothy's knee presses grew more demanding, he simply began to push himself against the arm of the couch.

And when the game ended, and the man placed his hands high on his and Jason's thighs and asked what they wanted to do next, Adam got up and said, "Well, *I* am going to clean up." He collected the plates and took them to the kitchen.

Adam could hear Jason and Timothy talking in the other room, but not what they were saying, due to the loud television advertisement. But then the TV switched off, and as he rinsed dishes, he heard, "Don't mess things up for me now, Jason."

"I'm not messing up anything," Jason replied.

"You *are*, man! If you weren't here, I'd have his knees on either side of his ears by now. Just like I used to have you."

"*Used to* being the operative words, *Timmy*."

"And don't *fucking* call me that! It's Timothy now. Or even Tim. I was *never* 'Timmy!'"

"You were to *me*" came the reply. And Adam could hear the hurt in it. "I loved you. You know that, right?"

"Which was why I broke up with you. I'm not a faggot!"

"Oh yeah? Then why'd you want to suck my cock all the time?"

"I… I was just being considerate. Doing something for you. I sure wasn't going to let you fuck me!"

I need to end this. It wasn't like he could leave.

"You almost did. Twice. But you said…."

Then he got an idea.

"Excuse me, my friends," Adam said, returning to the living room. "I hope I have not become the reason for this... remembrance of hurtful days past."

They stared at him, frozen as the statues Jason reminded him of.

Jason looked away, closed his eyes. Timothy stared.

"Hurting was the last thing I wanted. I wanted this to be a fun evening."

"Hell yes," said Timothy. "That's exactly what I wanted."

And there they were, right back to the subject of sex.

He would ignore it.

"Isn't that what we did? We had fun. I did at least. So much fun! And we got to know each other better. Or I, at least, got to know you both better. But I did not know that you had things unresolved. Pains still in your hearts. If I could leave, I would. But this is my home...."

Timothy gaped at him. "Wh-what?"

Adam looked back, feigning ignorance of what the man really wanted. Hoping his expression was one of pure innocence.

Timothy shook his head. "You mean you really thought that's *all* I wanted?"

Now Adam turned his performance up another notch. He pretended shock.

"Mr. Jeske. You don't think it's appropriate that we pursue more... personal matters while you work for me, do you? It would be most unprofessional. Someone *might* say I was paying you for more than your *carpentry* skills. That would be bad, wouldn't it? Think of your reputation. And mine."

Timothy looked down and spoke in a gravelly tone. "No one would know...."

"I would, Timothy. *I* would know."

He glanced quickly at Jason, whose mouth was slightly ajar, his eyes—of course—wide.

"And after the work is done?" Timothy asked.

"We will see what we will see." And then, although the ploy was beneath him, he offered Timothy a chance. He smiled. Let his eyebrows raise and fall in his most seductive manner.

It was a terrible thing to do, perhaps. Hint—strongly—at an offer he had no intention of keeping.

He looked at Jason. With whom he had a different goal entirely. Their eyes caught. He tried to speak of things unspoken. To make different offers.

"Oh for God's sake," Timothy said and crawled up off the floor. "I might as well go." He looked at the hole in the floor. "If I'm going to get this done tomorrow…."

"As you planned," Adam replied.

"Yeah. Yeah." He turned to the front door, then stopped and looked back. "Are there any of those beers left?"

"I believe I saw two," Adam replied. "But you must promise me not to drink until you get home."

Timothy nodded. He looked strangely shaken. It made Adam wonder about his story. What mysteries lay behind his eyes. "I promise. And I only want one of 'em anyway."

"No. Please. Take both. I enjoyed them, but I am more of a wine man myself." Indeed. He found himself yearning for the merlot, the 2011 in particular. He went and got the beers and handed them to Timothy, who took them with only a nod and then, strangely, left without a word to either of them.

Adam and Jason each let out what sounded like a long-held breath. They turned, looked at each other, and stepped forward, bringing them closer. Adam found his eyes honing in on those lips, wanting so to kiss them. The way Jason was looking up at him, breathing shallowly, mouth partially open, he was sure Jason wanted it as well, maybe even as much as he did.

Dare he think it?

Could it be true?

Could he have been deposited down in this tiny little village in the middle of a giant country and find a man he could love right there in his own backyard?

Jason took another step. Wet his lips.

And Adam made a crazy decision.

"I think," he said, "that you should go home now." It was the hardest thing he'd ever done.

JASON could not have been more surprised. He actually, to his embarrassment, gasped.

Adam wanted him to leave?

"But I thought…."

"I *do*," Adam said, taking another step. They were now *very* close. Jason looked up at Adam and longed for him to take him in his arms.

Kiss me, he thought. *Kiss me, please. It's been….*

"It's been *so* long," Adam said, echoing Jason's thoughts.

"Then… then why can't I stay?" He hated the pleading in his voice. The desperation.

Who wants a desperate man?

"I *want* you to stay," Adam said. "But I can't do this tonight."

"*Why?*"

Adam looked away. Then back. "For many reasons. Most of which I can't say right now."

Couldn't say? Why not? "I don't understand."

Adam reached out then and cupped his right cheek in his palm. "So beautiful," he whispered.

Jason tried to stand back but couldn't. Instead he leaned his face into Adam's touch.

"First, there is the matter of your old friend Timothy," Adam said then.

Jason scoffed.

"Jason. What if he is watching? I think he might. He seems the type."

"So what?"

"Well, first there's the matter of my living room!" He laughed. Or he tried to. It wasn't a very good laugh. "What if he gets so mad, he doesn't finish?"

Jason sighed. Then thought of a perfect answer. *I could leave and sneak back later*. But before he could say it, Adam said more.

"What if he sees and tells everyone?"

"Tell them what?" Jason asked. "Do you think I care if people know I'm gay? Pretty much everyone *knows* I'm gay already. Over the years, I've gotten them, bit by bit, to not give a shit." He pointed, with force, in the direction of his house. "Bit by bit, they've come to The Briar Patch and let me *feed* them. There are restaurants that *fire* gay employees for religious reasons—"

"Yes," Adam said. "The chicken sandwich place."

"—and because people will think they'll get AIDS because a gay guy touched their food. But I'm making it! I've got the elders of the town eating my food. The sheriff. I don't care if people start talking about me because of what Timothy might say."

"But *I* do," Adam said. "*I* care what people say about me."

He said it so forcefully that Jason fell back a step. Then, trying to help, he said, "Adam, I don't think anyone is going to care that you're gay."

"But it's not so much about that," Adam said. And now Jason heard a little of that desperation, that fear, in Adam's voice.

"Adam," Jason said. "What is it?"

Adam took a visibly deep breath. Let it out. "I'm not ashamed of being gay," he said. "I came to this country to *be* gay. There are so many things I gave up, people I had to leave… just to be able to be myself. There is no way for you to imagine…."

"Try me," Jason said. He didn't know why, but he was incredibly drawn to this man. It was more than his good looks, although he was indeed attracted to him. Jason didn't know what it was. He'd only known Adam for a day, but he'd already had an effect on Jason. Hell! He had it on everyone. He had Timmy—Tim—ready to fuck men again. He had Jason's mother inviting him to a family gathering after knowing him for only a few minutes. Adam had a powerful charisma that was almost impossible to ignore.

But it was more.

It was a quiet desperation.

Despite his cool, there was vulnerability. Jason wanted to get to know Adam. With a quiet desperation all his own.

"Give me time," Adam asked. "Give me time to tell you who I am and… and more. I could invite you to my bed tonight. Have sex with you. You want that, no?"

"No," Jason said. "I-I mean, yes! I do!"

"But would I be reading you right to say that I think you want more than that? More than what Timothy Jeske wants? More than fun? More than 'doubling up'?"

Jason let out a long sigh. God, yes! He wanted much more. He wanted it all. A companion, a lover, love. He wanted eagles sweeping down from Olympus. He wanted the fairy tale.

"I have done things I'm not proud of," Adam said. "Gave myself to…. No. If I told you, you wouldn't want anything to do with me."

"*Try* me," Jason said, placing his hand over Adam's heart.

Adam looked into his eyes. For what seemed forever. As if he were looking *for* something, and so Jason opened his eyes wide. Let him in.

Adam sighed. "I… I have given myself to men in the dark. Men whose faces I barely, and sometimes never, saw." Adam shivered, and Jason pressed his hand against Adam's chest. He nodded, wondering if he could bear to hear what the man was saying.

"I didn't *want* it that way. But it was the only way, my *only* way, to have a moment to be myself, a second's intimacy, a brief time to be with another man."

"Why was it the only way?" Jason asked.

Adam looked away, and this time, Jason took Adam's cheek in his hand. Turned Adam's face back to his own.

"Why was it the only way?" he asked again.

"Because of *who* I am. What I am."

"You're a man," Jason said. "A man who loves other men. Loves?" He left the remark with a question.

Adam nodded. "Who wants to love another man. Who wants so much more than an avventura in the dark. I want intimacy. I dream of waking in the morning and seeing the sleeping face of the man I love on the pillow next to mine. But every time I was with those men, it was like I was chipping away at my heart. Leaving little broken pieces of it behind me in the dark."

Jason's heart swelled at Adam's words. And nearly broke. "Oh Adam."

"I don't know if I have a heart to give anymore. But I'd like to find out if I do."

Oh yes, thought Jason. *Yes, yes, yes.*

"I don't want to find out in the dark," Adam said. "I am not ready to march in a Gay Pride parade. But I am ready to be in the sun. I couldn't do that at home."

My God, thought Jason. Adam's words made him want to cry. "Oh Adam," he said again.

"I want it to be like in the romance books. I want it to be like the movies. Like in the stories of the gods where Zeus falls in love and appears as a shower of gold, or sweeps down from Olympus as an eagle to claim his love."

This time Jason could not help but gasp. Those words! It was as if when Adam had looked into his eyes, he had also looked into his heart.

He was speaking of Ganymede!

"But I am not a god," Adam continued and placed his hands on Jason's hip. The gesture was electrifying. "I am only a man with a damaged heart."

Jason could see the statue on his dresser in his mind's eye.

"I have no wings—"

He could feel the crack in Adam's heart, in his own heart.

"—but I *must* fly."

Jason could see the desperation and fear and something more in Adam's eyes.

"I do not want my wings to be those of feather and wax like Icarus. I want to soar on wings of love." He sighed. "Maybe you think I am being silly. Perhaps you want to laugh at my naiveté?"

No! Jason started to shake his head but was stopped by...

"Yet, I think maybe, I *hope* that maybe, you are silly and naïve as well?"

He gave Jason a guarded smile. And looked at him with eyes filled with… was that hope? Jason thought so.

"Yes," Jason said. "Yes, yes, yes. To all of that and more!"

Adam smiled. It was the most beautiful smile Jason had ever seen in his life.

"Bear with me, then," Adam whispered. "With my secrets—that I will share with you when I'm ready. I promise. With my wish that everyone not speak of me—at least in rumors and wonderings. At my pace—which might be slow at first, but one day I will be ready to take your hand and run. Can you wait?"

Jason felt goose bumps shiver out across his skin. "Yes," he replied.

"I know it is naïve to hope that on my first days on your shore I could meet a man—you—to love so quickly. Maybe I have seen too many of your Hollywood movies. But it happens. I know it does!"

"I think so," Jason said, believed it.

"My parents met one day quite late in my father's life. They had both given up on love. But my father, he said he saw her eyes and his heart leapt. She said he held her, and she was his. He asked her to marry him after only one week, and they have been together for over thirty years. It happens."

"It happens," Jason said, feeling as if he were lighter than air.

"Wait for me?"

"God yes," Jason said.

And then, thank all the gods, Adam pulled him into his arms and kissed him at last.

Chapter Eleven

JASON staggered back home. He was high. He was drunk.

All from a kiss.

But oh, what a kiss! Gentle at first, like a butterfly. Then slowly, slowly, stronger, stronger still. Until Adam released his passion upon him. Stole his breath. And maybe—just maybe—his heart.

This had not been gasping and smashing mouths and stabbing, attacking tongues.

Did I ever think that was sexy? Jason wondered. And yes, the answer was yes. He had, until this day, thought kisses like Timmy's had been sexy.

Maybe they had been.

But now?

No. Not anymore. Adam's kiss was like life, like fire, like crashing waves that swept over him and took him under. When he had finally opened his mouth to Jason, it wasn't a challenge or a battle of lusts but an invitation. One impossible to deny. And when Jason accepted that invitation, Adam claimed him as his own.

Jason could not imagine kissing another man as long as he lived. Naïve to think, yes. But he knew it was true.

"I'm his," he said under his breath as he stumbled drunkenly home. He almost tripped going up the steps of his back porch and let out a little scream when Tim stepped out of its deepening shadows.

"Jesus Christ!" Jason cried.

"Sorry, Jason," Tim said, blinking at him through heavy-lidded eyes.

"What do you want?" Jason asked, heart still in his throat.

Tim held out the two beer bottles with his right hand. "Well, that we share these first." He took two big steps toward Jason, bringing him close, "Then a little of this…." And then he brushed his hand across the crotch of Jason's pants.

Jason's mouth fell open in shock.

"And then some of this." Tim reached around and grabbed Jason's left buttock firmly in his big hand.

Jason was shocked into immobility. But when Tim leaned in to kiss him, that paralysis was instantly broken. He reached up and pushed Tim back. "What are you doing?" he asked.

"You know what I want! At first I thought he was just trying to get rid of me so he could have you to himself. So I waited outside and watched. But then a few minutes later, you came out—"

Well I'll be damned. Adam was right.

"—and unless he's the quickest fuck in the world, he's left you just as blue-balled as me."

Tim stepped back into Jason's personal space. "Come on, Jason. You have to be as horny as I am after that."

"Oh I do, do I?"

"Don't you miss it?" Tim asked, voice heavy with lust. "*Us?* I know I do. God, we were good when we got naked."

Jason could not have been more stunned. "You called me a faggot," he blurted.

The beer bottles slipped from Tim's hand as if forgotten and luckily, even though they made some noise, they didn't break.

Tim sighed. "I-I know. I… I shouldn't have done it. But I was with my friends. And they were…. I was afraid they were figuring me out."

Figuring you out?

"I was trying to throw them off."

Throw them off?

"I'm sorry, Jason. I'm *really* sorry."

Now with both hands free, Tim reached around, took both Jason's asscheeks, and gripped them hard.

"Come on," he said. "Give me some of your honey pot. You know you'll like it."

Jason pushed Tim back harder. "Stop."

Tim did. But he looked at him seriously now. "Please, Jason."

Jason gulped. "You're engaged Timmy…. *Timothy.*"

"You can call me Timmy. I just didn't want you to say that in front of Adam."

"Go home to Sally," Jason said.

"You're making me beg? If you want me to, I'll beg. Please let me fuck you, Jason."

"Go fuck your *fiancée*, Tim."

"It's not the same," Tim whined.

"*Why* isn't it?" Jason moved to push Tim again.

"Because…." He looked away.

"Because what?" Jason asked.

"B-because…." Tim started to look back, but then turned his face away again.

"Yes?"

Tim faced him. "B-because…."

"Tim?"

"She doesn't have a penis, Jason." Tim covered his face with his hands. "She doesn't have a *cock*!"

Jason gaped at Tim in astonishment.

"Oh God, Jason!"

"Timmy?" He'd never seem Tim like this before. And had he just said what Jason thought he'd said?

"What am I going to *do*?"

"Tim," Jason said and took his wrists and pulled at them. "Look at me."

Tim lowered his hands enough to uncover his eyes. He looked as if he were about to cry. "What am I going to do?" he said in a voice Jason could barely hear.

"About…?"

"Cock, Jason." Tim's eyes were all but bulging. "Oh, Jason! I *love* it. I love cock. I can't get enough of it. I want it *all* the time. I need it all the time. I can't stop thinking about it. What the hell am I going to do?"

Wait… a… minute, thought Jason. *What is Tim saying?*

"Timmy…. You've been…. You've been…."

"Yes!" he cried, and God, was Tim crying? "I've been sucking cock."

"B-but…. But where? How?" This was one shock upon another.

"You'd be surprised at h-how many dudes want to. Just not with girly men. Or nerdy men like…." He stopped.

"Nerdy men like me?" Jason asked.

"They see a *man* like me, and that makes it okay, I guess. Less…."

"Nerdy? Or faggy?"

Tim looked away again. "There's this bookstore about an hour away. An *adult* bookstore? Th-they have these booths where you can watch X-rated movies. And some of them.... Oh God, Jason... some of them have holes between them."

Glory holes? Tim was talking about glory holes?

"Guys... they stick their penis through the holes and...."

You suck them, Jason realized.

Tim covered his face again. "They stick them through, and I'm like... I can't stop. It's like I'm addicted."

And you can be. Sexual addition is a very real thing.

"It's a fucking miracle I haven't gotten herpes or the clap. What if I took that home to Sally?"

Suddenly Tim dropped his hands, and he raised his eyebrows high, grinned a weird kind of grin, and nodded his head quickly.

"But Jason! *You* could help me stop *doing* that!"

"Me?" Jason shook his head. "How can I...?"

"I can go ahead and marry Sally but have you to take care of my other needs. And you wouldn't be all alone anymore, 'cause you'd have me on the side."

"Me on the side...," Jason echoed, astonished at this new development.

"Exactly!" exclaimed Tim. "It's *perfect*."

"Except that it's not," Jason stated flatly.

Tim looked confused. "It isn't?"

"No," Jason said, feeling very sad.

"Why not?" Tim asked, that desperation returning.

"Because I don't want to be your dirty little secret."

"My-my what?" Tim looked even more at a loss than before.

"I'm ready to walk in the sun," Jason said. "I'm ready to walk down Main Street, Buckman, holding another man's hand, proud of who I am."

"Are you *crazy*?" Tim backed away. "Do you think people are going to stand for that? This ain't San Francisco!"

"Some people won't like it, I'm sure," Jason replied. "But most won't care at all."

"You *are* crazy," Tim snarled.

"Maybe I am," Jason admitted gleefully. "But I'm in good company!" And he thought of Adam. "So go home now, Timmy."

No. Not Timmy. *Timothy*, he thought, and made the conscious decision to leave Tim behind at last. To close the door on that part of his life. To say goodbye.

It felt... good.

"Just go, Timothy. I can't help you."

He unlocked the back door and was stepping inside when Timothy took his arm again. He looked at Timothy sharply.

"Jason," said Timothy quietly. "*Please.*" Pleading. "Just this *one* time. It could be our goodbye."

Jason sighed. But knew he couldn't be subtle about this. "I've already said my goodbyes, Timothy." He gently pulled his arm from Timothy's grasp.

"Huh?"

"And closed my door." He stepped through his doorway then, turned, and as he closed it, Timothy cried out.

"I'll let you fuck me!"

Jason froze.

"You always wanted to. We tried twice, and I bailed on you. If you give me one more night, I *will* let you fuck me. You'll be able to say you had my cherry!" Timothy smiled, his mouth an awful rictus.

And in that frozen moment, was he tempted? He'd given nearly everything he could to a boy named Tim. Including his heart. But Tim had kept one thing back.

Didn't he owe Jason that? Wouldn't it be wonderful to finally experience what *Timothy* was offering?

But then he thought of Adam again.

He couldn't give Adam his virginity. But he could save that one last thing. Wouldn't it be wonderful if the first time he experienced being inside a man, it was Adam?

"I'm sorry, Timothy. I can't."

Again, he started to close the door, and again Timothy stopped him.

"It's him, isn't it?" Timothy said.

And again, Timothy had startled him.

Was it?

Was the reason he could turn Timothy down because of the sweet possibility that was Adam?

He couldn't deny the possibility was sweet. But no. He thought that he'd reached the place in his life where he would have said no to Timothy's offer if he'd never met Adam. He most certainly didn't want to be some kind of mistress. And he couldn't live with himself for helping someone cheat. How would he look at Sally the next time she came into the Patch for her allotment of Harlequin romances? Why, he was already going to have trouble looking her in the eye just because of this, wasn't he? His stomach dropped at the very thought of it. Her all happy faced and totally innocent of what the man she loved was up to.

"It is, isn't it?" Timothy pouted. "You want to be with *him*."

No. This wasn't about Adam, although the mysterious sexy man had certainly helped him get to this point in his life. In less than twenty-four hours!

But sometimes life turned on a dime.

And this turn meant he truly was ready to walk in the sun.

He shook his head. "I'm sorry, Timothy."

"This is revenge," Timothy cried as Jason quietly shut the door. Then loud enough so he could still hear: "You want him. You think he's better than me. With that snotty I'm-better-than-you faggy accent!"

Faggy accent.

And there it was, wasn't it?

Timothy declaring he was addicted to giving men blowjobs, but he could still say words like faggy. As if the word had nothing to do with him.

There was more after that, but by then Jason was climbing the steps and couldn't make it out. He considered working on his novel, and would have if it hadn't been for Timothy. The drama had made him way too unsettled to write romance. So he went to the little bedroom he'd turned into a living room of sorts and turned on his television—a flat-screen but so much smaller than Adam's—and he watched a movie he'd been meaning to for some time now. A gay romance of sorts called *4th Man Out*. He loved it. It made him feel all warm inside. Made him feel the world was full of possibilities.

And he couldn't help but think of Adam.

When the movie was over, he brushed his teeth and undressed. Thank God, by the time he sat on the edge of his bed, there was only silence outside. He wondered if Timothy was still out there.

He looked at his statue of Ganymede and felt a little rush.

He looked out beyond it to the light still burning in the little house behind him.

He smiled.

And then he got under the covers and fell almost instantly asleep.

He had very pleasant dreams.

Chapter Twelve

THE call came right at 8:00 p.m., as planned. Which meant poor Cristiano was making the call at three in the morning Monterosia time. But his brother, head of Monterosian Security, said it was the most unlikely time anyone might notice that the Skype call was being made. "A prince has vanished. People are going to be looking. It's going to be chaos, my brother."

Despite Adam's feeling of guilt about that, especially what might happen to Cristiano if it was discovered that he'd helped Adam, it was so good to see his brother's face.

"How are you, Adam?" Cristiano asked right away—no fanfare.

He smiled. "Good. Despite a few surprises, I am very good."

Cristiano frowned. Of course he did. "Surprises?" he asked.

Adam shook his head and waved his hand to brush away his brother's concerns. "It is not for you to worry yourself about. It is nothing. I wanted a bike, now I must ride it. If these things are all I have to worry about then I am a lucky man. Now tell me…. How are you? I worry you're in trouble."

Cristiano looked at him in that way of his that said he wasn't done yet, but after a sigh, he answered, "I am fine, Amadeo. Everything went according to plan. It could not have gone better. Even I am surprised. No one has even hinted I had anything to do with your disappearance. Not even Mother, and you know she can see right into our heads."

Which was true. They had never been able to get away with anything as children. Which is exactly what he said to Cristiano.

"Of course," Cristiano answered, "when we were boys, I didn't have the resources of the entire security measures of our country. I had no idea how to use a hundred different methods to cover up what I did."

"Like the time we crawled down the ivy from our rooms and went down to Roccaforte to hang out with boys?"

Cristiano rolled his eyes. "*Santo cielo!* And when they found out we were smoking marijuana, I thought they would die. I was so ashamed. And the boys!"

Adam nodded. "I thought they were going to put them in a dungeon!" The palace didn't have a dungeon, but there were times he and Cristiano were convinced that it did.

His brother laughed. "Sometimes I still wonder, despite what I know, if there is a dungeon Father has not told us about."

"I was just thinking the same thing!" Adam laughed with his brother. "And that you might wind up shackled to a wall." It felt good to laugh.

Cristiano sighed and shook his head. "No chains." He held up his hands to prove it. "But Oddio, brother. What have we done? This is far crazier than sneaking off to try pot with the town boys. Everyone is so upset. So worried!"

Adam's heart sank. "Oh, Cristiano. I…." He swallowed hard. "I am so sorry."

Cristiano shook his head. "No. This is important. I only wish there was a better way."

New guilt rushed in. "Mother? Father?"

His brother sighed. "That is the worst of it. She is totally distraught. Worried you're dead. Father worries it is a foreign nation, and you've been kidnapped."

Kidnapped by a foreign nation? A country as small as ours?

"Cristiano. We have to let our parents know that I am all right."

His brother sealed his mouth tight, then nodded in agreement. "I thought that you would say so. But know that sets in motion events that will leave a footprint that might be used to follow you back to where you are."

"And also mean you, Cris, could be revealed to have helped me get out of the country and set up a life here." It was a hard decision to make. He did not want to get his brother into trouble. Not after all he had done. Including and perhaps most of all, support him when he found out Amadeo was gay. Especially the way he found out.

"All right, then," Cristiano said. "I want you to write to them. I will send you an email telling you where to send your email. It must be different than the ones we have already set up. Reveal almost nothing.

Say simply that you had to get away and that you are alive and well. Understand?"

"Yes," he said, knowing also that Cristiano could very well—perhaps should—edit what he wrote.

"Can you get this to me by this time tomorrow?"

"Of course. I will work on it as soon as we sign off."

"We will decide what to do from there," Cristiano said. There was a long pause. Then Cristiano continued, "I hope this is what you wanted, Amadeo. I hope this… running away from home is worth it."

For once Adam wasn't sure of Cristiano's meaning. Was this an angry accusation? A "see what you've done?" Or did he truly hope that this crazy thing Adam had done was the right thing to do? He decided to believe it was the latter.

But how to answer? How to let Cristiano know that maybe, just maybe, Adam might already be on the threshold of everything he'd ever wanted. That it was crazy. But that crazy might be something wonderful. And even if he was being silly and naïve to think that Jason might be who he was looking for, he was also mature enough to understand that even if Jason wasn't what the Americans called "Mr. Right," he could very likely be the best and most wonderful "Mr. Right Now" there could possibly be. Because for the first time in his life, even living in a shoebox in the middle of nowhere, he was doing what everyone had the right to do: pursuing love. Maybe even making mistakes.

He would not let Jason be a mistake. Whatever happened, he would not be a mistake.

And he found himself wishing Jason hadn't gone home. That he was still here. Right here. Just the two of them.

"You're smiling," Cristiano said.

"I am?" He reached up and touched his mouth without thinking about it, as if he could feel a smile. "I'm smiling?"

Cristiano's brows raised. "Amadeo, what are you not telling me?"

"N-not telling you?" Adam asked. What in the world? And then, unbidden, Jason filled his mind, and he realized—*well, I'll be*—he was smiling.

"Amadeo?" Cristiano was leaning toward the camera on his computer, and his face filled Adam's laptop screen. "Spit the toad! What's going on? What are you not telling me?"

"N-not telling you?" *Oddio!* What was he *not* telling his brother? That he'd met a lovely young man almost immediately and was harboring silly unrealistic fairy-tale wishes that he'd already found who he was looking for? He would think Adam was being ridiculous. Childish. Naïve.

Cristiano's eyebrows rose even more, and his eyes went wide. Adam couldn't help but think of Jason. "Amadeo! You can't have found someone already? Could you? Did you?"

And to Adam's surprise, there was no look of reproach. Nothing scolding. No criticism at all. But then, why would there be? This was Cristiano. His brother. Who had been the one who had come to his rescue when he'd been arrested. Somehow kept the *Polizia di Stato* from realizing who he was, kept it out of the papers, kept their parents from finding out…

"THIS is not the way for them to find out. Thank God you left your wallet in your hotel room."

In the car, Amadeo sat for the longest time, gathering his thoughts, trying to figure out how to bring up what had happened. Finally he simply said, "Don't we need to talk about this, Cristiano?" and was terrified what his brother would say.

"What is there to say?" Cristiano asked in return.

Another very long pause. And when he built up the courage to respond, "Are you ashamed of me?"

Cristiano turned to him as fast as could be. "Ashamed? Why would I ever be ashamed of you?"

He'd never been so close to having an emotional breakdown as he was in that moment. "So many things, brother. That I am homosexual—"

Cristiano cut him off. "Amadeo, I've known you were gay for a very long time."

Amadeo's mouth dropped open in response.

"You *never* looked at the girls. I wondered about it, and then once when we were watching the Olympics, I saw how your eyes never left the television screen whenever they were showing the swimmers. The male swimmers. I saw it in your eyes. That's when I began to suspect. Then when I go to visit you in college in Rome and I met your roommate, I knew for sure. Your eyes, brother. You have never been able to lie to anyone, especially me. And eyes do not lie."

"B-but why didn't you ever say anything?" Amadeo asked, astonished.

"Because you were not ready to speak of it. And because at the time I didn't know much about homosexuality. I thought like many people that it was a phase, you know? I mean... I fooled around a bit with one of the stable boys when I was fourteen."

Amadeo's mouth fell open. "You *didn't!*"

"Of course I did. It is normal. And then—"

"Who," Amadeo demanded.

Cristiano laughed. "That, my brother, is none of your business. The point is, with me, it is how they said. I grew out of it. I was with him because I was a horny young man. And when the girls came around, I was only too happy to make their acquaintance. That was when I noticed that they never interested you, despite how much they were interested in *you*."

"And you are not ashamed…?"

"I told you, Amadeo. I could never be ashamed of you. But I did worry about you. I wondered what would happen. I wondered when you would come to me about it. But you never did. And I am only sad that more years had to pass and it had to come out between us this way."

There was a long silence after that. And then slowly they began to talk. Cristiano asked him what he was going to do? And Amadeo said he supposed that he would marry, the way so many gay men did. What else was there to do? He was the heir to the throne. Monterosia wasn't ready, and probably would never be ready, for a gay crown prince. If for no other reason than he had to have an heir.

"Will you be happy, brother?" Cristiano asked him.

"I'm not happy now, Cristiano. Why else would I degrade myself to meet with men in alleys? To give my body that way to some stranger?"

The shame came back then, and oh, his brother showed his unconditional love when he shot back with, "No, Amadeo! Do not talk about yourself that way. You wouldn't have done what you did unless you felt you had no choice. Do not curse yourself. I curse a world in which my brother cannot be who he wants. And somehow, dammit, I will help you find a way."

WHICH was how he'd wound up here, sitting in front of his little laptop in a tiny town called Buckman, skyping with his beloved little brother in his equally beloved Monterosia.

And it was why Cristiano was not looking at him as if he were foolish, silly, naïve…. Gods. He looked happy.

"Amadeo? Tell me?"

He grinned. "I don't know. But, Cristiano! I have already met two gay men." Thinking about it, he sobered. "One who is ashamed of himself. Who is engaged to a woman and who sneaks out for sex with other men." *That was me. And who I promised to become. Hiding myself from everyone, including an innocent wife….*

"And the second one?" Cristiano nodded, smiling, urging him on. "Tell me."

God! He was excited. Which made him forget all about scenarios where innocent people were hurt. "The second one…." Suddenly he felt as if he had had one too many glasses of wine. He grinned foolishly, and his cheeks heated up. "Oh, Cristiano! He is about the most beautiful man I have ever met. And we have a connection. I think we do!"

Now Cristiano was grinning a huge silly smile, and that made Adam even happier. "And?" He wagged his eyebrows. "This connection? Have you two…?"

Adam's face went from warm to hot. "Not yet. I asked him if he minded waiting."

Cristiano looked at him, an expression of surprise on his face. "You *did?*"

"Yes, brother," he said. Then lowering his voice, shame peeking at him from around a corner, awaiting its chance to sweep over him once again, he added, "Just because…." *Just because you found out I have had sex with men in alleyways doesn't mean that is the kind of sex I want.* "Just because I have not waited before doesn't mean…."

Then, completely ignoring Adam's implication, Cristiano said, "*Beeello!* This is wonderful. You big romantic you."

Shame died in its corner. Adam found himself grinning again.

"Oh, Amadeo! I so hope this happens for you. It will make it worth it, no? Don't you think?"

"I hope so too, Cris. I hope so too. But whatever happens, I am living for the first time in my life."

"Then no matter what happens, here and also there, I am happy for you, big brother."

After that Cristiano reminded him to write his letter as fast as possible and to send it to the new email address. They wished each other well and finished with saying how much they loved each other.

They signed off, and Adam sat there on his bed, thinking about how he might be on the edge of doing what he'd said to his brother. Truly living.

Then he thought of writing the letter to his parents. A sense of dread filled his stomach.

But then he thought of love.

And let that guide his words.

> Dearest Father and Mother,
> Let me say first how much I love you. I wish that I were a poet so that I find the words to express myself. But that was never my forte. So instead, simply know that I love you.
> Second, let me try to apologize for what I have done. Know that I had my reasons. Know that it took me a long time to make this decision. Know that I feel that it is

the only choice, in the end, that I could make. The only option I saw that could work.

I am alive. I am well. And I am happy. Oh, Father! Oh, Mother! I am *so* happy. And I have only begun!

I cannot say any more at this time. I promise you that I have not vanished forever. I will contact you again. I might even tell you where I am. But I ask, I beg, that you not look for me. Not yet.

You have been the perfect parents. But we don't always live in a perfect world. I am simply looking for a place where I can find the closest thing to perfection I can.

I love you with all my heart,
Your Amadeo

He sent the email to his brother before he could think too much more. His brother would make any changes that needed to be made. And if he allowed himself to, he could worry and fret all night about his letter.

Better to let it go and pray for the best.

He went to bed then, but in no time he saw that he was not going to be able to sleep. When he closed his eyes, his mind became like the gusting winter bora, the winds that in northernmost Monterosia could simply blow you away if you didn't hold on to the chains set up along the walkways. When he closed his eyes, there were no chains. Only those 200-kilometer winds.

Adam got up.

He opened a bottle of wine, since he'd given Timothy the last of the beer, and was glad of it. As it turned out, the bottle he'd picked wasn't bad. Not at all.

He was drinking that first glass when his eyes fell upon *Down from Olympus*. Jason's book. He picked it up. Reread the blurb on the back. Then went back to his bed, since he didn't want to settle on the couch in its hole in the floor. He tried not to worry that Timothy by Demand would not come back to fix it and turned to the first page of his book.

The first paragraph drew his attention…

> Sean was a man alone. And
> not just on the sandy beaches of
> Santorini. He was alone no matter
> where he was. Alone abroad. Alone
> with friends. Especially alone in
> his tiny hometown of Cranbury,
> where he knew he could never allow
> anyone to know who he really was.
> He was gay in a place that would
> never allow him to be gay. And
> therefore, he was alone.

Sean was a man alone. *Gods*. Adam knew the feeling. He looked at the cover again and saw Jason's name. He touched the letters with a fingertip. *Are you alone too, Jason?*

Adam read on…

> And even on this beautiful beach
> where once the gods looked down on
> from their high places and turned not
> their eyes away from men who loved

men—in fact some of them loved
male mortals as much if not more
than the female—a lifetime would
not allow him to give up his feelings
that he would always be alone. That
he would never find love.

Adam read late into the night.

IT was an old dream, and one he had not had in years.
Later he would assume that the stranger-in-a-new-land
that he'd become brought it on. But now it was simply
the dream, as strange as it was real.

He was fourteen, leaving boyhood behind and
becoming a man. In some cultures, he would have been
considered a man already.

The palace was dark, most everyone asleep, and he
was playing, avoiding guards, running from curtained
alcove to suit of armor to statue of hero or god. He had
just ducked behind one of his favorite effigies when,
to his surprise, his father and two other men swept by,
cloaks swirling around them, actually carrying torches,
although they were unlit. The only light was that of the
full moon shining through the great windows on this
side of the palace.

Rashly, he decided to follow them. Slipped off his
shoes and went silent as a cat behind them. They walked
for some time until they came to an alcove that looked
scarcely large enough to hide one full grown man, yet
all three dipped inside… and did not come out.

Amadeo waited a moment and then tiptoed to the place
where he'd last seen his father. But to his astonishment,
neither his father nor either of his companions was visible.

He stepped in and gave a gasp at the big stone bull's head looking down at him. He had seen it a thousand, thousand times and not a few of them at night.

But *this* night, the eyes glowed.

How could that be? Adam climbed up onto its knees, the only part besides the head that jutted out of the wall, and the glow vanished.

Damn, he thought. He was sure he'd seen it. He shifted his head then and—oh!—they glowed again. You must only be able to see it at the right angle. He turned this way and that—light on, light off—and then reached up to investigate, to touch them. A slit appeared, accompanied by the rumble of metal and stone shifting, and then the bull slid back into the wall!

Amadeo was in a hidden corridor. It sloped down from where he stood, visible in the glow of a strange orange light. Shouts and cries and chants echoed in the distance, and...

Then he woke, sweating, afraid, and he didn't know why.

Chapter Thirteen

THE sun rose on another glorious Midwestern day. Jason chose the small section of porch at the back of his house to have coffee with his sister. Not that he didn't like his front porch. But the house sat on Main Street and didn't allow for much privacy. Privacy was what he wanted this morning.

Besides, it allowed him to look at the warm dun-colored house where Adam was probably still asleep. Maybe he would step out onto his back patio—his piazza. Wouldn't that be nice?

"This is so mysterious," Daphne said. "Like something out of one of your books." Then she continued in her best 1960s television narrator voice, "Jason Brewster was a gay man living in the tiny town of Buckman, where nothing ever happened. That was until the mysterious stranger moved into the small house behind his. A house that had stood empty for years…."

Jason rolled his eyes.

"Okay! So I'm not the writer in the family. But still, you have to admit, it is mysterious."

"Thesaurus your 'mysterious,' Daphne."

She rolled her eyes. "*Such* a nerd."

Jason took a drink of his coffee and looked out over his iris plants to the tiny house behind. *Come on, Adam. You can do it. Step outside. I want to see you.*

"I mean, maybe he's a spy," she said, eyes bright.

"A spy." He said it flatly. He didn't even question mark it. The suggestion was that silly.

"Well," she replied, "where do guys like James Bond go when they're not on a mission or fooling around with Pussy Galore or Holly Goodhead? Maybe he goes to little British villages like Dibley or Pagford, where nobody knows him…."

"Or Midwich?" he offered, not looking her way. *Come on out*, he beamed at the little house. *And I'll give you some real coffee.*

"Huh?" she asked. "Mid… which?"

"Never mind," he said. He leaned back in his bright aqua directors-style chair and picked up his coffee.

Daphne shrugged. "I just think there are all kinds of cool possibilities."

"*Hmm…*" was all he said.

It only seemed to spur her on. "Maybe he's a defrocked priest. Maybe he did something sexual, and the Vatican sent him as far away as possible so that no one—"

Jason sat up. "You're not suggesting…?"

"No!" She held up a hand. "No, no, no." She grimaced. "No, I was thinking the whole gay thing could be it. Like maybe he had a mad affair with a bishop or a cardinal or something. I don't know. Maybe *he* was the bishop or whatever!"

"He didn't really strike me as the religious sort."

"I guess he wouldn't with his whole 'I want to do you, but let's date first.'"

"Is there anything wrong with that?" Jason snapped. It was nice to see someone might want to get to know him before sex. Wasn't that why he'd run out on the last couple of chances? All they'd wanted to do was hop in the hay.

"Not at all," she said, reaching out and touching his hand. "Tom and I haven't gone all the way yet."

He raised his eyebrows.

Hers came together when she saw his look. "I'm serious. We've necked, but that's about it."

He didn't lower his eyebrows.

"*And* I let him touch the girls," she said and crossed her arms over her breasts.

He continued to give her the same look.

"I mean it! I like him, Jason. Quite a bit. Because he's not harassing me into going all the way right off the bat."

That was possible. He nodded.

She sighed. Looked away. When she faced him again, she said something that surprised him. "I'm scared."

Scared? he thought. Daphne? Scared?

"It doesn't hurt a guy's reputation when he sleeps around."

"Unless it's with another guy," he said.

"But with a girl, she becomes persona non grata. Or a slut. Especially in a town like ours. I haven't been with anyone since He Who Shall Not Be Named."

Meaning her high school sweetheart. Who went away to college and came back with a pregnant wife.

He sighed sympathetically. That had hurt her badly. He figured it was a big part of why Tom Rucker was the first guy she'd considered having anything to do with in years. "We're quite a pair, aren't we?" Jason asked.

Daphne sighed and rested her chin in an upturned palm. "Yeah, we are, aren't we?"

There was a long pause as each drank their coffee, lost in thought.

But then "Maybe he's in the witness protection program...."

"Daphne!"

"Well, why not? Maybe he witnessed a gang hit, and they've got him hidden away. Maybe he ratted on some Tony Soprano guy. You know? And now he's here in Buckman so they don't ever find him. Because geez, who would think to look for anyone here?"

"I thought you wanted to live, get married, have kids, and die in Buckman," he said.

"I do," she said. "But that doesn't mean I think we are the action capital of the world. You're the one with dreams of going to Chichen Itza so you can fall in love with the human personification of Kukulcan."

"Greece," he corrected her absently. "So I can fall in love with Zeus."

"But he's *old*," she moaned.

"So are all the gods," he said. "They're thousands of years old."

"I could almost believe you're serious," she said.

At times, he almost believed it himself. The idea that some god would make him a cupbearer had its fascination. But in the end he realized there was only one thing he wanted. A real flesh-and-blood man. Someone to live with.

Marry.

Grow old with.

"Maybe he's married," Daphne whispered.

"Who?" Jason asked, absently.

"Adam. Maybe he's married to a duchess or an impossibly rich someone, and he's realized he's gay and he's come here to be himself. Ran out on her...."

"God no, I hope not," Jason said and was surprised to feel a pang of pain. "Not married."

"Maybe he's set up a little nest so he can play with boys now and then, and then he can go home to her."

"Please, Daphne. Don't say things like that."

That was when Adam came out of the back door of his house. Jason froze. "There he is," he whispered, all thoughts of wives and bishops and spies forgotten.

"He is fit, isn't he?" Daphne whispered back.

Fit? He wanted to laugh. It seemed like such a clinical term. Hot is the word he would have used.

"He's gorgeous," Jason said.

"Ian Harding gorgeous," she confirmed.

Jason nodded, watched as Adam came through the little gate. *What's he doing?*

"You know I think maybe even Charlie Hunnam gorgeous," she stated.

"Adam isn't so... scruffy." He narrowed his eyes, saw that Adam was now walking around the backyard, bending, standing, bending. Was he weeding? "That is more Tom Rucker's domain."

"I mean Charlie when he's all cleaned up," she clarified. "Like when he's going to some movie premier. Not when he's being all *Sons of Anarchy*, 'violence-is-inevitable,' Charlie."

Jason barely heard her.

Because.... God... it looked like.... God! He was! Adam was coming this way. "Charlie is ruggedly handsome even when he's cleaned up," he said, barely able to contain his excitement. "But Adam? Adam is beautiful. And here he comes."

"Charlie Hunnam?" she asked, eyes wide.

"Adam Terranova," he responded as Adam arrived. He had flowers.

And he was holding them out to Jason.

"*Buongiorno*," Adam said.

"Holy crap," gushed Daphne.

ADAM was startled when he saw the intense blue flowers, what he knew of as *fiordaliso*, growing along the gravel alley behind his house. He'd always loved them, and they'd become a bit rare in his country. Apparently not so here in the state of Missouri. This made him happy to add them to his bouquet, along with gold and pink snapdragons, white daisies, and a few orange poppies—the last of which of course reminded him very much of home. He only thought they were beautiful. Like Jason. So why not take them to him?

And he couldn't help but smile when he saw the beautiful man sitting on his back porch (almost as if he had been waiting for him) as he walked the seventy-five feet between his home and Jason's. But before he could say anything, tell Jason just how he felt, Jason's sister said something first.

"Holy crap." Her eyes were wide, and she was staring.

The words took him by surprise.

"Daphne!" Jason cried.

But then she said, "Flowers! Tom's never brought me flowers!" She turned to her brother. "I swear, Jason, if you botch this, I'm never going to let you forget it!"

Adam's smile was back. He brought his feet quickly together and bowed ever so slightly—in that way his mother had taught him—and held the flowers out to *l'oggetto del suo desiderio*. The object of his desire. "They pale in comparison to you, but this is my offering. I hope they please you."

Jason looked as if he might cry. He didn't move. And sadly didn't reach for the flowers.

Adam lowered the flowers. "I did wrong?" he asked.

"You most certainly did *not* do wrong!" said the sister. She elbowed Jason. "*Take* them, silly!"

This seemed to awaken Jason, and he opened his mouth, shut it, opened it, and shut it again—saying nothing. He did, however, hold out his hands.

"He says, 'thank you,'" Daphne said.

"Ah—y-yeah," Jason said. "I mean, yes. I mean...." He took the flowers and brought them close. "No one has ever brought me flowers before. I... I didn't know what to say. You took me by surprise."

"It is a good surprise, then? Yes?"

Jason's cheeks went deep pink. "Oh yes. Thank you." He sighed. "Thank you *so* much."

After a brief silence, Daphne asked if he might like to join them. "Since my brother isn't asking."

"I think that is his choice. Right? That is the proper thing for me to—"

"No!" Jason gasped. "I mean, please! Please join us." Then, "Hey. You can try American coffee."

The idea interested him. How it would compare to Monterosian coffee, which was world famous. Although Jason was obviously unaware that the coffee Adam had brought from home, and it had been a small amount, was in fact famous. At least to the rich and famous. It still disappointed him that Jason hadn't liked it. He climbed the few steps and sat at the little black wrought-iron table, while Jason jumped to his feet. "I'll be right back!"

Adam nodded and then glanced at Jason's sister, who was smiling at him like a Cheshire cat. He couldn't help but be a little nervous.

"You have to excuse my brother," she said then. "He's a bit shy. And today, nervous. It's been a long, long time since he's liked a man."

Adam swallowed hard. "And… Jason. Do you think he likes me?"

"And how!"

"And how?" he asked.

She nodded, resumed smiling. "Yes. He does. A *lot*."

The news was like sunshine breaking through a dark gray day. "You make me happy with these words," he said. "I like your brother a lot as well."

"He said you kissed him like he's never been kissed. He said he didn't dream he could be kissed like that."

Adam looked at her, stunned. Then his heart skipped. Not only because of what Jason had said about their kissing. But because he was talking of this openly. With a *sister*. It seemed almost impossible to believe. They were speaking as if this were as common as asking how much the olive oil he wanted for his pasta would cost or what he thought of the weather. It was *bravissimo*! He felt like weeping for joy.

Jason was back then with a lovely clear glass vase and the flowers—*bene*!—and—*santo cielo*!—an enormous cup of coffee. It was light in color, so he knew that Jason had added cream. But how was he supposed to drink this much? He wouldn't sleep for days.

"Thank you so much for the flowers. I just don't know what to say…. Wait. Are you crying?"

"Only from happiness," Adam replied.

"And on that note, I think I'll go inside and see what I can get ready before we open," Daphne said and was on her feet and gone before Adam could do the polite thing and ask her to stay. Then he smiled. He couldn't help it. He was glad she was gone. He wanted to be alone with Jason.

"I could not sleep last night thinking of you," he blurted, and then gasped inwardly at his brashness.

Jason smiled his beautiful smile, and any worries were banished. "Should I say I'm sorry?"

Adam shook his head. "No." And then he did another rash thing, since the last one had been forgiven. Or perhaps liked. He reached out and touched Jason's hand. Jason had seemed to like it before. And then— oh!—Jason turned his hand over, once again exposing his palm. Adam immediately let his fingers rest there.

"Timothy was here when I got home. He was watching the house like you thought he might."

He was? Timothy was here. To his surprise he felt a jolt of jealousy. "And?" he couldn't help but ask.

"He actually wanted to have sex with me."

And? But this he couldn't ask. He swallowed hard once again. Tried not to let Jason see his inner struggle.

"I sent him away, of course."

Adam let out a sigh of relief before he could help it.

Jason's eyes flashed. "You didn't want him to stay?"

Now Adam narrowed his. "You tease me, Jason."

Jason bit his lower lip.

"I think that two men who are thinking of becoming lovers should not tease." Again, was he too forward by saying that? Too brash? Too soon? He had never courted anyone.

Jason nodded. "I'm sorry. You're right. We—*I* shouldn't have teased you."

Because? Adam asked with his eyes.

"Because two men who are thinking of becoming lovers shouldn't tease each other."

Adam's heart swelled to near bursting.

"At least not that way," Jason said and smiled again.

Adam took Jason's fingers in his. Squeezed ever so slightly. "Oh Jason." He couldn't believe how his heart was pounding. "Is there anyone I have to ask permission to *corteggiare*... to court you?"

"You can ask me," Daphne said from the doorway. "And I say yes!" She nodded and ran back into the house.

They laughed then, and for Adam it was joy, joy, joy. He felt like a teenager. He didn't know if he had felt like this with Salvestro, his college lover. Had he? It was so long ago it was almost like it hadn't happened. But this. This was now!

Finally, absently, he took a drink of his coffee and.... What in the world? He looked down into the full mug. Had Jason made some kind of mistake?

"What's wrong?" Jason asked, looked very concerned. "Is there something wrong with the coffee? You like lots of sugar, right? And...."

"Yes...." Adam tried not to grimace. "But...."

"Oh God! I didn't put salt in it by mistake, did I? How horrible! Here, let me go get you another cup and—"

"No!" Adam held up his hand. "No salt. No worries. It is just that this coffee.... Maybe you did make a mistake, but... it wasn't salt."

Now Jason looked curious. "I don't know what you mean. It's the same pot I'm drinking from. Might not be the same cream. Maybe I gave you some spoiled cream?"

"No," Adam said again. "It's not *schifoso*, um…. Come si dice…? How do you say in English…? Gross? Bad? It is not that…."

"Here, let me." Jason took the cup. Held it to his face. Nodded. "Do you mind?"

Now Adam nodded. "Please." If Jason tasted it, then he would understand.

Jason sipped. Got a curious look on his face. Yes, so he would know what was wrong with—

"It tastes fine. Except that I don't usually put sugar in mine and only cream when it's really strong. But this tastes fine."

Fine? Really? "It doesn't taste long to you?"

Jason's eyebrow raised. "Long?"

Adam nodded. "Yes."

"I don't understand. How can something taste 'long'?"

Now Adam was confused. Long…. How did he explain it better? "The coffee I made you. It was 'short.'" He held up thumb and forefinger an inch or two apart. "Short. But this…." He lifted the coffee mug and with his other hand spread his thumb and forefinger as far apart as he could. "Short? Same amount of coffee beans but way too much water?"

Jason's eyes went wide, and then he burst into laughter.

He's laughing? I said something funny?

"W-weak?" Jason said and wiped at his eyes. "You think it is weak." The latter being a statement and not a question.

Adam nodded. "Yes. Very. It is more like muddy water."

Jason started laughing again. "Oh God! That is so… so… funny!"

"Why?" Adam wanted to know. "What is funny?"

Jason stared at him and started laughing again. "B-because I thought your coffee was way too strong, and you think mine is too weak. It's hilarious."

Adam saw it and smiled and then laughed himself. "It was funny."

"Do you think it is too high and wide a bridge to cross?" Jason asked.

"What do you mean?" Adam asked.

"The difference in our coffee. Because coffee is the liquid of life. Mankind must have his morning coffee? How will we ever make it work if you want that tar you drink—"

"*Tar*?" Adam exclaimed. His coffee wasn't tar!

"—and I want to drink 'muddy water'?"

Oh! Now he saw. He started laughing again. But only for a moment. Then he grew serious. He reached out and took Jason's hand in his. "It is never too high or wide a bridge for me to cross to find a way to be with you."

Jason froze. His mouth opened and closed. Then he very quietly said, "Gosh." His mouth opened and closed again, and his eyes went glassy. "No one has ever said anything like that to me. I never dreamed that anyone would ever say anything like that to me."

Adam smiled.

Jason smiled.

They stared into each other's eyes and—

"And I hate to break this up," said Daphne, suddenly reappearing and making them both jump. "But the Patch is going to open any minute."

Jason and Adam sighed at the same time.

"Now, I can open, no problem. There is only one person at the door—"

"Sheriff Ryan?" Jason asked.

"—and I can serve coffee—yes, of course it's the sheriff—and the quiche is ready, and I can boil water, but...."

Adam stood. "Then I should leave," he said, now gripping Jason's fingers.

Jason stood. "Maybe we could have dinner tonight? I could make…. Damn. The bridge club is meeting here tonight."

Daphne sighed. "I can take over for that."

They turned to her as one. "You could?" they chorused, to Adam's secret delight.

"Why the hell not? It's not like *I'm* doing anything. Tom is in Arkansas." She put her hands on her hips. "Just don't let this become the way things are, okay?"

But her eyes were sparkling.

Jason hugged her. "Thanks, sis." Then he grimaced. "Well, crap."

Now what? Adam wondered.

"Yes?" Daphne asked.

"I can't very well make dinner for two with the bridge club here—"

"I will take care of that!" Adam said. "Hopefully there will be no hole in the floor. But either way, I will make you a meal like Cook made for me!" And the very idea set his heart afire.

"I would love that," Jason said and stepped close to Adam.

Adam stepped closer. "And that's my cue!" And Daphne was gone.

This time Jason kissed *him*. He raised his head and wrapped an arm around Adam and kissed him.

Adam's pulse raced.

This kiss was not as long or passionate as the one last night. It was hardly the time or place. But there was always tonight….

They parted with that promise.

It was one of the happiest days he could remember.

Chapter Fourteen

ADAM got home just in time to let Timothy in. Asked him if he minded if Adam went to the store for some groceries. Timothy was quiet, almost cold, but not rude. It was a relief. He hadn't even been sure Timothy would show up. But then he had a reputation to keep, and "by Demand" was the one that made him money.

He was lucky to find a little roadside stand only blocks from his house on the way to Walmart. That was where he got his tomatoes and onions. Big, lovely things that smelled like heaven.

Finding everything else he wanted wasn't that easy. Luckily there were only a few snags.

Pasta he found. Olive oil as well, including a few brands that looked quite promising. The beef wasn't difficult, and it was nice and fatty, which made for a tastier stew. The bread was a bit of a problem. He wasn't happy with what they had and finally settled on french bread and hoped it would be good. But then, beggars couldn't be choosers. It would work. It was then a happy accident that he stumbled onto frozen bread that needed to be baked. He never imagined such a thing. Bread was made daily; everyone knew that. But then the french bread had hardly been made today, had it?

He wished there was a lady in curlers to ask. When he asked an employee, she seemed to be as surprised as he that Walmart carried frozen, unbaked bread.

It was the seasoning that frustrated him the most. They didn't have much in the way of fresh spices and herbs, and he loathed using dried. Then to his surprise, when grumbling his frustration aloud, an older man said, "Why don't you check the garden department?"

"Excuse me?" Adam said. He hadn't realized he had been talking out loud until that moment.

"Yeah. Sure. It's that time a year. I bet they got some. I know they have basil 'cause the old lady loves it. Buys a ton every year."

So Adam made his way to the "garden department" and was thrilled the moment he walked into the caged-in, open-to-the-sky section of the store. There were plants everywhere. His nostrils flared at the purity of growing things, and a deep nostalgia hit him—but mostly, thankfully, in the loveliest of ways. He found rosemary and thyme as well as the basil the old man told him about. He didn't need basil, but he got it anyway. Why not add herbs to his garden?

He had to buy the dried marjoram and bay leaves but considered himself lucky. Didn't Cook use dried bay leaves anyway? He bought the most expensive ones, in hopes it meant something good, and got paprika while he was at it. They had organic paprika, which made him happy, but that was how it was listed—as paprika. It did not mention if it was hot or sweet. And the one sweet type he found did not mention if it was organic. *So frustrating.* If he were at home, he'd simply go down to the market— well, with royal guards of course—and taste whatever he wanted from the big heaps of spices on display. Not because he was a prince. It was how everyone shopped for food.

Frustrating, frustrating, frustrating. He would have to order from the internet in the future.

Then to his utter joy—silly how such a simple thing could make him so happy—he found a hot Hungarian paprika by someone called McCormick and prayed for the best. So he had both kinds.

Finally, a wine.

Walmart was not a winery. He was going to have to do something about wine.

But his last try hadn't turned out badly, so he stood for ten minutes and wrestled with whether to get another merlot or a zinfandel. In the end, he went with zinfandel from Silver Springs Winery and once more wished for the best. The *aperitivo*, though, was a loss. They didn't have Campari to make Negroni, so he went with little tiny cans of spritzers from a winery with the unlikely name of Barefoot. He could only hope there as well.

When he got home, he started to work while Timothy made lots of noise in the living room. Adam was surprised to see how far he'd come.

First he cut up the onions and tomatoes, some for the goulash and some for the third course. Then he added olive oil and some white vinegar to what was going to be the last course and put it in a bowl in the refrigerator.

The longer they were together, the better, as far as he was concerned. Then he cut the beef into cubes.

But then there were hours and hours before Jason was to come over. What should he do?

He smiled.

Finish *Down from Olympus*, of course. He was loving it. The mixture of reality and mythology sent his imagination soaring. Wonderfully, Jason was leaving it to the reader's imagination whether the gods were real and alive and involved, or whether it was all just coincidence.

He decided to believe the former.

Because even though he was raised Episcopalian and prayed to God like a good Christian boy, there remained that other side of him. He poured the first bit of wine out for the gods. Sometimes he swore to them. And often he thanked them. He looked off toward Italy, toward where Olympus should be, and it was easy to imagine them. Easy to picture Zeus on his throne. Easy to see Apollo in his mind's eye. Easy to see Ares too. And do the things he should to appease them....

He knew he wasn't the only one. Hadn't he heard both his father and brother swear to and by the gods? At least when Mother wasn't around?

It was comforting. They seemed so much closer and more real—with their lusts and their loves and their mistakes and gallivanting and broken hearts—than the Christian God who was so.... He didn't know. Best not to chance that god's anger by thinking such things.

He forced himself to stop reading when he reached the last chapter and went inside for two reasons. The first was to check on Timothy's progress.

He was shocked at what he saw. He had a floor!

It wasn't a gorgeous floor. It wasn't a dark, stained-oak hardwood floor with layers of finish. It wasn't even pine. It was the kind of floor meant to be covered with carpeting. But that was all right. It really was. Interesting how soon he was finding comfort in all the ways this place wasn't a palace.

He was down from Olympus. He was seeing why the gods became human.

And he liked it.

"*Oddio!*" he exclaimed. "*Beeello*! Look at all that you have done!"

Timothy, who had been frowning when he came in, cocked his head, stood up a little straighter, and wound up grinning. "Well damn…!" Now he was grinning. "I try my best."

"I will tell everyone of your work!" Adam kissed his fingertips and then let them fly outward from his face. "*Eccellente!* I had nightmares that this would take weeks to do!"

"Well, I told you I would be done today. I think I can have everything done except the carpet by four this afternoon. The carpet by five or six at the latest."

Adam grinned at him. "You are a miracle. *Grazie!*"

"Well shit…." Timothy shuffled his feet. "Thank you."

"Before I go back out onto my piazza, I am going to my room to place an order on the internet. I want to stay out of your way."

"You need my help in there?" Timothy asked, and he bobbed his head toward the bedroom.

"No, I will be fine for now. And I very well might have more work for you. That roof for instance. Can you get to that this week? I would hate a storm to ruin the work you have done."

The look of disappointment was unmistakable. But Adam chose to pretend he didn't notice. "Yeah. Sure. Thursday work for you?"

"It works wonderful!"

They shook on it, and then Adam went and logged onto his laptop to do the second thing he'd planned. He looked up Jason's publisher. And found that he had one other book. Only one. Damn. He ordered it, though. Got it in paperback and found that meant he got an e-version as well. Which meant he could read it on his computer while he waited for the other to come. He had a feeling he would be finished before it arrived.

To imagine his Jason, his *amato*, could write like this. It spoke of a man who knew about love.

After that he went back outside and finished the book, and he loved the ending. Loved that mysterious beings, one of which he knew had to be Cupid, looked down from the mountains and congratulated themselves on a job well done. It was the gods!

And maybe, just maybe, the gods were at work for him and Jason? Were the two of them human? Or gods themselves?

He checked the clock and—oh! He needed to start the stew so there would be time for it to slow cook. He set his cook pot on the small oven—it still looked like a toy to him—and wished he had gas instead of electric. But as the old saying went, *hai voluto la bicicletta? Allora, pedala!* You wanted a bike? Now pedal!

He poured a bit of olive oil into the pot and then stir-fried the onions. Then he added the beef and did the same, browning it and filling the house with its wonderful aroma. He dissolved the paprika in a little water and poured that over the meat. Next was the tomato sauce, some tomatoes he hadn't already set aside, and the salt and pepper. Finally he added the dried herbs and then picked a sprig each of the rosemary and thyme and put

them in last. Once the whole thing was bubbling, he
stirred it well and lowered the heat to a simmer.

In two hours, it should be done. All he had to do
was check it periodically and see if he needed to add
any water to make sure the stew didn't get dry.

Now he simply had to wait.

Sure. That was all he had to do. Wait for Jason to
arrive and all that implied—all that could happen and
how they might know when to make things happen?

But there was no knowing *now*, was there? All
he really could do was wait. So. Allora. Why not start
reading Jason's other book?

And that's exactly what he did.

THE meal was delicious. Jason was amazed at how
delicious.

He showed up with a bottle of wine, even though
he'd been told not to. "Bring nothing," Adam said to
Jason after their kiss. And boy, he couldn't believe
he'd had the nerve to kiss Adam. It had been the most
impulsive thing he'd ever done.

But he still brought some wine. It was the way he
was taught. He hoped the merlot from Silver Springs
Winery would go with whatever Adam had made.

He'd knocked on the front door this time, and
seconds later the door opened, and there stood Adam,
looking so gorgeous, so light-years beyond gorgeous,
that he hadn't been able to speak. His breath and words
had simply been taken away.

It was Adam's turn to wear white, it seemed. Jason
had steered away from it because Adam was Italian, and
that could mean spaghetti sauce. Everyone knew you were

jinxed whenever you wore white and ate Italian. No matter how careful you were, you got red sauce on yourself.

Adam seemed not to have heard this or wasn't worried about it.

And he looked like something other than human. That was how lovely he was.

"Prego, entra! Please, come in!" He opened the door.

For a second Jason was frozen. But the glory of Adam's smile allowed him to move. Because, wow, did he want to go in.

Inside there were candles. Candles everywhere. And look. "A floor!"

"Yes," Adam said and chuckled. "A floor. But if you do not object, we will still eat out on the piazza."

I don't mind anything *you want me to do. Just name it!*

"Something smells delicious," Jason said. The wonderful smell of cooking things filled the air, and he found he was salivating. He'd been so nervous the last few hours, he hadn't even realized he was hungry.

"Now I told you not to bring anything," Adam said, pointing to what Jason was holding like a life preserver.

"What?" Jason asked. "Oh! I brought wine." He held it out.

"Grazie," Adam said. "You did not need to." But then there is always room for wine. He looked at the bottle. Smiled. "I almost bought this. It was like a flip of the coin." He looked at Jason. "Thank you, Jason." And he said it so deeply and warmly and genuinely that Jason was almost dizzy.

And then Adam kissed him. It was only a brush of his lips, first over either cheek as he lightly hugged him, and then, just as softly, on his mouth. But it sent his heart zinging.

Please have that be a preview of things to come, Jason thought.

In the candlelight Adam looked even more beautiful. His slacks as well as his shirt were white, and he was almost luminous, like some kind of angel in the warm glow. He was wearing a light blue casual jacket that seemed to be just thrown on, as if he wore such clothes every day. Who knew? Maybe he did. And white shoes. Gods. Simply *gorgeous*.

Adam motioned for Jason to come farther in. "Please. *Entra, entra!*" Then he directed him to the couch. "Please. Sit. Plenty of room without Timothy by Demand."

Candles sat on the coffee table, along with what looked like a plate with rolled-up pieces of meat and… yes, olives.

"You see," Adam said with a Vanna White–like gesture (although Vanna was never as beautiful as Adam), "I have antipasti…."

"*Anti*pasta?" Jason asked, giggling inwardly and thinking, *Like the Antichrist?*

"You call it hors d'oeuvres or… like the appetizers?"

Jason nodded. He'd known that of course, seeing what was there, but it still made him giggle.

He sat and, at Adam's urging, leaned in to look at the plate. Big fat green olives without the pimento or, he suspected, the big seed. Little mini pieces of bread—bruschetta?—with what looked like ham and pale cheese. And rolled-up meats like salami and ham. The latter turned out to be *very* salty, and Jason supposed it was all on the salty side. Perhaps to make a person hungrier?

It certainly made him want the spritzer Adam gave him to go with it. He really enjoyed it. He had two and wished he could have a third. Meanwhile, Adam made frequent dashes to the kitchen. It didn't allow them a lot of time to talk. But that was okay. No jumping into the deep end!

He disappeared once more and this time for what seemed forever, although Jason knew it couldn't have been more than a few minutes. When he came back, he was smiling.

"Signore, your table awaits." Adam held out a hand and helped him to his feet. He led him through the kitchen, where you would never guess a dinner had been cooked except for a few pots and—oh, look there—a colander filled with steaming pasta sat in the sink. Otherwise the kitchen was spotless. Jason's kitchen never looked like this.

Adam opened the back door and stepped through— there was no room for Adam to step aside inside the kitchen—so that Jason could pass him. Once he was outside, Jason's eyes widened in surprise. What he saw was simply lovely.

More candles. Many, many, many more candles. They were everywhere. Small votive candles were placed along the picket fence. Larger candles sat on every possible box or bench and even on a trash can. And the table, complete with a white tablecloth, held three candlesticks and a bottle of wine. It was like something out of a movie. It near brought tears to Jason's eyes.

He went to the table and then was surprised when Adam held the chair for him and scooted it in after he sat. From seemingly nowhere, his host produced a white linen napkin and offered it over an arm. Jason took it and placed it on his lap. Music was playing, and when he looked around, he saw a cell phone glowing nearby. It was playing "One of These Nights" by the Eagles. He smiled.

With a whoosh, Adam was back, this time with a big plate of the pasta. Strangely, there was no sauce on it. After vanishing and returning once more, Adam placed what could only be fresh-baked bread and a bottle of olive oil next to the plate. "For you to choose how much you want," he explained.

On what? The bread? But if so, Adam hadn't placed a traditional small plate on which to pour the oil.

Once more Adam left and then returned with his own plate. "You didn't need to wait for me," he said, motioning to the olive oil. And then he did something a little… odd before he poured their wine. He went to the picket fence and poured just a bit onto the ground, almost as if it were a libation. Before Jason could really think about it, and without explanation, Adam was back at the table and filling their glasses. "You do drink wine, yes?"

Unbidden the line from various Dracula movies flashed into his mind. "I never drink… wine." Everyone knew those words. Funny, it never appeared in Bram Stoker's book.

I am such a nerd….

When the glasses were full, Adam raised his. "To possibilities," he said.

Jason nodded, and they touched glasses and then drank. It was nice. Very nice.

Then after a pause, Adam asked, "Is something wrong?"

"I'm… I'm not sure." Jason gazed at the pasta. Steam rose from the bowl with a tantalizing aroma. "Aren't we missing something?"

Adam looked at the table. "Oh! Scusi! The salt and the pepper!" He leapt gracefully to his feet and zipped in and out of the house as before, very quickly, and placed the condiments next to Jason. "Now you are ready? Nothing missing? Oh! I could get butter, but it is not our tradition for bread with dinner like this. Is that all right?"

"Spaghetti sauce," Jason said, almost too loud, and wondered if Adam was joking with him. "There's no sauce."

For a second Adam didn't say anything. And then his eyes flew wide, and he laughed and said, "Scusi," once again. "Ah, the part of Italy I come from, we don't traditionally use sauces whenever we serve pasta—which is every meal. Usually we use olive oil. Lots and lots of olive oil! Here. Let me."

"You don't use sauces?" Jason asked. Why, wasn't spaghetti sauce as Italian as… well… spaghetti? It was used in every movie he ever saw. Even *Lady and the Tramp*, although that one wasn't set in Italy, was it?

Adam took the olive oil bottle and poured it over Jason's pasta. He gulped. He wasn't sure. "Here. You try, okay? Then tell me if you want more?"

So, with not a little reluctance, Jason started to cut a section of the pasta and—

"No, no! Here. Like this." And Adam poked the fork down into the pasta and turned it until he had a huge bite. He raised it and held it to Jason's mouth. "You try?"

His face was eager, and Jason couldn't refuse him. Thought he would never refuse him anything. He opened his mouth, and Adam slowly slid the forkful in, and it occurred to him in that instant what an erotic moment this was.

He closed his lips, and Adam slid the fork back out and looked at him, eager as before.

So Jason chewed.

And—*my God!*—it was delicious.

"Wonderful," he said after swallowing.

Adam's eyes danced in delight. "Beeello!" he cried. Then, "Mangia! Eat up." He sat down, poured twice as much olive oil on his own pasta, and began to wolf it down. He would nod between bites and say, "See? You don't need the red or the white sauce. You have olive oil. The food of the gods!"

And it was good. Jason had to admit it. The food was very good. Just different.

"Oh, è così buono!" Adam rolled his eyes in pleasure. "*Buonissimo!* Proprio come lo preparano a casa!"

Jason smiled through a mouthful of pasta and after swallowing remarked, "I don't know what you said, but I am guessing it is how much you like the pasta?"

Adam nodded. "Basically, I said it was very good and reminded me of home."

"I love your language so much. I think it is the most beautiful I've ever heard. It makes my heart... I don't know. Flutter."

"Some people say that French is the loveliest language," Adam said.

Jason shook his head. "I don't think so."

"I do not either. But then I am... prejudiced? Right? I used that word right?"

Jason laughed. "You did." He took another bite. "I think Italian is so poetic. The cascading rhythms.... Beautiful!"

Adam got the oddest expression on his face then. Sad maybe? Not what Jason would have expected.

"You move me," Adam said. "You remind me of what I take for granted. I am glad you love my language."

But somehow Jason thought there was more. Almost... pain. Maybe Adam was just missing Italy?

"Say something to me again," Jason said to keep the mood happy. "Something in Italian. *Italiano!* I don't care what. Anything. Say 'the quick brown fox jumps over the lazy dog.'"

"Why would I want to say such a silly thing?"

Jason laughed. Shrugged. "I think *anything* is beautiful in your language."

And there! That almost hurt look. Why? But then he grinned, rolled his eyes. "Yes. Well. Let's say that it's difficult to have your dog obey you in Italian."

Jason burst into laughter.

Adam leaned forward. Rested his chin in an upraised palm. His smile went soft. Sweet. He looked into Jason's eyes. "Hai gli occhi più belli che abbia mai visto," Adam said. And, "I fiordalisi impallidiscono al confronto con i tuoi bellissimi occhi."

Jason trembled. "Gosh," he said. "I take it that has nothing to do with foxes?"

Adam shook his head. "Nor lazy dogs." Then before Jason could ask. "I said that you have the most beautiful eyes I have ever seen. And that the *fiordalisi*—you call them bachelor's buttons—pale in comparison to your beautiful eyes."

Jason rocked back in his seat. Forced himself not to gape. And suddenly there were tears. He fought them, but they were building. He could feel them filling his eyes. He didn't have a clue what to say. His thoughts were numb. Then he blurted, "That is the first thing I thought about your eyes when you finally took off those damned sunglasses of yours." He wondered why he was now making light of the situation. A wonderful man had compared his eyes to the intense blue flowers that grew between their properties. "Daphne thought you might be a vampire or something—until I reminded her the first time you two met it was a bright sunny morning."

Adam's gaze grew more intense then. "*Sei incredibile*, Jason," he said in a soft—and God, sultry—voice. "Sei bellissimo. Sei *la mia rosa*...."

Suddenly Jason found he couldn't talk about vampires. Or Daphne. Or even be silly at all. Adam had taken his very breath away. Again.

Then Adam's eyes became even deeper. More powerful. Passionate. "I said you are incredible, Jason. That you are beautiful. You are my rose."

"Gosh. Oh my. I…." He couldn't speak. He couldn't put together a coherent sentence.

"I *want* you to be my rose. Will you think about it?"

"I…. Oh yes," he said and was aware he was gushing.

Adam didn't seem to mind. He reached out and took Jason's hand.

A SECOND course followed the pasta. It was a delicious stew. Jason couldn't believe how wonderful. It was what had filled the house with such a delicious aroma.

"You like?" Adam asked, eyes filled with eager hope.

"Yes!" He laughed. He felt so fantastic. "It is…." He didn't know any Italian, did he? "*Wunderbar*," he said, trying to make it sound exciting, rolling letters he didn't even know if he should be rolling.

"Grazie," Adam replied. And, "Maybe I can teach you Italian?"

"Oh, I would love that!" he exclaimed and meant it.

"You know I read your book," Adam said then.

Jason's fork stopped midway to his mouth. "Already?"

"It is not like I have much to do," he said. "And I could not put it down. I *loved* it."

"You did?" He grinned, unable to help but be pleased.

"I loved your heroes. My heart could not help but go out to Stanley and Dominic. And I loved how they have a connection with the ancient gods. I couldn't help but wonder if this was something you simply researched, or if you also feel something...."

"A *connection*," Jason whispered. "I can't help it. My mother. She raised me with those stories. Of Jason and the Argonauts, and the labors of Hercules. The story of Medusa and Pegasus, and Theseus defeating the Minotaur."

"Yes!" Adam said excitedly. "Except that it was my father. He tells the story of my people, that one of the very first of our people defeated a kin of the Minotaur. But my mother is devoutly Episcopalian and gets nervous about people talking about the gods as if they were real."

"Is that why you poured out some of your wine before serving us," Jason said, titillated. "Was it a libation?"

Adam looked a bit embarrassed but then sat up straight. Proud. "Yes," he said. "Some think it foolish and—"

"My mother has done that my whole life," he said. "In fact she has these statues of Jupiter and Diana and Juno on her dresser. She leaves them offerings. Candy and money and honey wine. We aren't Italian as far as I know. She declares herself to be Methodist. She won't talk about them, but Daphne and I aren't stupid." Jason felt his heart pounding. "This is amazing. I've never been able to talk about this."

"It is common in Mont—" Adam stopped. "In the mountains," he finished. "Even today. My people, they do the same. And when she doesn't know I am watching, I have seen my mother leave flowers at the statue of Juno out in the gardens."

"She loves you," Jason said, something stirring inside him.

"Oh?" Adam said. Urging him on?

"Juno. She is the goddess of women and children, right?"

Adam grew even more animated. "And marriage...."

"Yes, but the flowers were left for *you*, don't you see? If it was for her marriage, she would have left something like wine, wouldn't she? No." Jason was gearing up now. Other than Daphne, he'd never dared bring up these thoughts with anyone, not even Todd, who was a *Star Wars* geek. Certainly not Timmy—*Timothy*. He wouldn't have been able to comprehend what Jason was talking about in their high school days. But with Adam... why... this shit was real! Or at least was something worth talking about.

"Your mother wasn't taking any chances. She prayed for you in her church. And she left an offering asking Juno to take care of you—"

"And Cristiano," Adam added, all but cutting Jason off.

"Cris... te... ano?" Jason asked. Who was...?

"My brother." That cloud came over Adam's face again but then was whisked away as quickly as it came.

"I didn't know you had a brother," Jason said.

"I—I am sorry, Jason." The cloud again!

Jason shrugged. "We barely know each other. There's *lots* of things we don't know. That's what this is *really* about, right?" He motioned back and forth between them. "Getting to know each other?" The cloud was gone again.

"Yes."

Adam smiled. Then, "It is just that my brother is very dear to me. We are *very* close." He held up two fingers and crossed them. "Like this. And I felt there that I had *denied* him. I didn't like that feeling."

"Well, now I do know," Jason replied, and then he reached out and tugged at Adam's intertwined fingers, and before he knew what he was going to do, Jason kissed those fingers. A shiver rushed through him. He wasn't used to doing such impulsive things, and he couldn't help but wonder what Adam would say.

Any worries were gone when Adam sighed and pulled Jason's hand to his own lips. "I *like* this getting to know you," he said. "Tell me everything about you, Jason Evander Brewster. And I will tell *you* everything that I can."

Chapter Fifteen

ADAM lay in his bed staring up at the ceiling. He couldn't sleep. His mind was too full. It all swirled around, and each thought wrestled for attention to be the chief thought on his mind.

Jason. How much he liked Jason. Liked the way he looked. Liked his voice. His personality. The way he laughed. The way his thoughts moved from one to the next. How very much he liked getting to know Jason and how each thing he found out only made him want to discover more.

And his eyes! Oh, his eyes. How they reminded him of the blue of the Mediterranean.

His lips. What heaven it was to kiss those lips! Oh, how he wanted to breathe from Jason's lips. Drink from them.

And who was he fooling except perhaps himself in saying that he "liked" Jason Brewster? He no more "liked" Jason than he *hated* him. He thought perhaps "love" was the word, and a hair's breadth from falling *in* love with him.

And therein lay the rub. How could he fall in love with a man he was lying to? In getting to know Jason, he was lying about himself.

He had come *so* close to saying "Monterosia" and changed it at the last second to "mountains."

A lie.

How many other lies had he told? If not downright lies then the lies of omission? Letting Jason *think* something and not correct him? Wasn't that still untruth?

But he couldn't very well say, "Buongiorno! I am Amadeo Montefalcone, the prince of Monterosia," could he?

He hadn't thought this through. He wanted to come to America to meet someone with whom he could fall in love. And then, hopefully, build a relationship. But how could he do that if it was built on a foundation of lies?

They had been having such a good time. How they'd laughed while eating the third course of tomatoes and sliced onions marinated in olive oil—when he'd told Jason the dish usually was served with cold octopus "which I was not able to find at Walmart." Jason had thought he was joking, and when he'd realized that Adam wasn't, his eyes had gone their widest yet. Adam had started laughing, and then Jason joined in.

"It's not like I haven't heard of octopus," Jason said once he'd calmed down to a final few snorts. "Sure I have. But I decided it was one of those things like chitlins or menudo that I just didn't need to try. There's plenty of things in the world to eat, like your amazing stew, without eating animal cuts or tentacles!"

When Adam asked what "chit-lins" and "moo-new-due" were, and Jason explained they were the intestines of a pig and beef stomach, Adam decided to have a little fun with him.

"Well, we eat some of those things," he said, keeping a straight face. "For instance, we have a dish called *cervella fritte,* which is bite-sized batter-fried morsels of beef brain. It is... what did you say? Wunderbar!"

He had to dig his fingernails into his palms to keep looking serious. "And it sounds like *lampredotto* is similar to your menudo. And *pajata* is—"

"Stop!" Jason cried, and then Adam lost it. He started laughing, and when Jason saw he was teasing him and rolled his eyes and giggled, he was simply adorable.

"Actually, all those things are real food," Adam said. "They are eaten in Italy. But in... my part of the country"— another place he'd almost said his country's name—"the region I came from, only the poor eat stomach and intestines. But... seriously now, my father *does* love *pajata.*"

"Which is?" Jason asked, looking more than a little disgusted.

"It is intestines of veal that have not yet been weaned from their mothers, so their bellies are filled with milk. It is creamy and cheery and—"

He saw the sad expression on Jason's face, and his heart melted.

"—and I refused to eat it as a kid and have never tasted it since. Mother says I cried whenever Father ate it, so he finally gave it up for Lent one year."

Jason pouted. "Poor baby cow."

Oh, Jason was *adorable.* Poor baby cow! One more reason he found himself so deeply drawn to him.

After dinner, Adam usually would have had coffee, but he knew how that had gone over, so he made one for himself and then watered down a second for Jason.

It apparently was a failed experiment, and when he explained what he'd done, it only caused more laughter.

Oh, the sound of Jason's laughter! Almost childlike. And so full of happiness. It made Adam's skin tingle.

"I cannot believe I'm sitting here laughing in the open air with you," he told Jason. "You do not know. I couldn't do this at home. Anyone who saw us, any waiter, they would think we were lovers. And that would cause a lot of trouble."

How lovely that Jason's eyes grew wet. It made Adam's heart pound.

A very romantic song began to play then—John Legend's "All of Me"—and he asked Jason to dance. Jason nodded and rose, and when Adam took him into his arms, Jason said he didn't really know how.

"I will show you," Adam said, and Jason let him lead, and for the first time in his life, Adam danced with a man.

It was a very powerful moment. Adam felt as if his heart *really* was in his throat. He also could not deny how erotic it was, and he got hard, and as he wondered what Jason might think about that, Jason grew hard against him. And so they danced, their hard cocks riding side by side, and Adam grew wet and knew soon it would be able to be seen.

He stopped, as did Jason, and then Adam kissed him. Slowly at first and then more and more urgently, Jason taking Adam's lead in a different kind of dance. And just as he became convinced he would have to take this man to his bed…

Michael Bublé's song "You Don't Know Me" began to play. Adam heard the lyrics, heard Michael sing about the taking of hands and the beating of his heart, and how the object of his affection thought he knew him but didn't know him at all....

And he saw the shining trust in Jason's eyes... and he couldn't do it.

"Jason?"

"Yes" came the reply, Jason's voice cracking like a teenager's, although Adam had found out that evening he was twenty-five to Adam's twenty-nine. That trust was the final strike.

"I—I think you should go now, *luce mia*."

Jason trembled. "Wh-what?" Clearly surprised.

Looking into those amazing eyes, Adam saw that he had hurt Jason, which in turn hurt him. He did not want to cause hurt in the man he was indeed falling in love with. But so fast! This almost instant love... could it be real?

Then he remembered something his father once said to him. The memory filled his mind so suddenly, so fully, he almost gasped.

"You will know it's love when it strikes swiftly." His father struck his chest with an open palm. "Cupid's arrow to your heart! It almost *hurts*! That is the way it was with Caterina, your mother."

Adam had never seen his father with such a... beatific expression on his face. So often his father seemed impassive. Royal.

But not on that day.

"Now I loved my first wife. I did. But I *grew* to love her. The marriage was arranged. We didn't even meet until weeks before the ceremony. But I did fall in love with her. Deeply. And by the Christ, I loved our

children. I was devastated when they died in that...."
His voice faded. The hurt was still so clearly there. His
father continued, whispering now, "The flames... I see
them in my nightmares."

His father rarely talked of his first family. Adam
knew his father had been married when he was a very
young man, and his wife and two children had died in a
tragic accident, their car going off a cliff.

The king had refused to remarry. He said he could not
put himself through that again, and the people despaired
that there would never be an heir to the throne.

"And then... by Venus... your mother. Her eyes! I
fell into her eyes and then into love. *So fast!*"

He struck his chest again, this time with a fist.

Then he looked at Adam, his eyes brimming. "*That*
is how you will know."

Adam looked into Jason's eyes, and he gasped. He
was falling into them. And he was falling in love.

"Did I do something wrong?" Jason asked then.

"No! Gods no!" Adam cried.

"Then why do you want me to leave?"

"Because if you do not, I will take you to my bed."
And that would be wrong.

"I want you to," Jason said eagerly.

But how could he make love to Jason when Jason
did not know who he was?

"I cannot," he said then, and it was the hardest
thing he'd ever done.

"But I want—"

"Please, Jason. Let me do this the way I need to
do it." Adam touched his chest. "The way it should be.
When the moment is *right*. Not when our bodies want
us to. But when our hearts say they cannot wait another
instant!"

Jason sighed. Nodded. "But I'll see you tomorrow?" he asked, a certain desperate tone in his voice.

"Of course," Adam said, even though he was already beginning to make a decision.

ADAM lay in the dark, staring up at his ceiling, thinking of his father striking his chest and saying, "*That* is how you will know." Thinking of the absolute trust in Jason's eyes. Thinking of how he was lying, even if it was only by omission.

He had to make a decision. He either needed to tell Jason who he really was—and how could he do that?—or stop seeing him.

And so he made a vow.

He could see Jason no more.

Chapter Sixteen

BUT when Jason showed up at his door the next morning, Adam's resolve crumbled immediately.

"Hey!" Jason said, cheerful as a child. "I got this *great* idea!" And before Adam could ask, he went on, "You're a citizen of Buckman now. I should give you a little tour. And since the Patch closes at two today, I can take you around. Show you the sights, such as they are, of course. Buckman isn't Manhattan."

Adam smiled. "It sounds delightful. And I am not sure I would like your Manhattan anyway."

So that's what they did. Jason drove, and the vehicle was not what Adam was expecting—a big, beat-up tan pickup truck. It made Adam feel so... country.

"Now this is Main, I'm sure you've got that figured out," Jason said and began pointing out different businesses. Most of them were redbrick, but with fancy facings. "What's sad is how many of these old buildings are empty. I mean, look at them. These are historical landmarks as far as I'm concerned. See there? On the sides of some of them?"

Adam looked and saw the faded remains of… ads. One for Pepsi and another for something called Sinclair Gas.

"I love that. They've recently repainted one, which I wasn't too crazy about. I think they should have left them like they were, but"—he shrugged—"that's the way it goes."

Adam noticed then that Jason was right. Quite a few of the storefronts were dark, no merchandise in the windows, some soaped over. "Why are they empty?" he asked.

"Walmart," Jason said in something akin to a growl. "Those superstores come into a little town like Buckman, and all the small businesses just dry up and blow away. They can't compete with their prices. Not only the mom-and-pop places that have been here for years and years and years, but even stores like Ben Franklin. My aunt was a manager there for years. Now they're all gone. And Walmart's not the only one. We had this amazing video store with really cool selections you just can't find anymore. Then Blockbuster moved in, and the place couldn't survive with the big chain's deals going against them. So the video store fails. A year or two later, Blockbuster goes out of business, but my favorite store is already gone."

Adam couldn't follow a lot of what Jason was saying because the culture was so unfamiliar. Ben Franklin? He thought Ben Franklin was some kind of founding father of this country. And he had no idea what Blockbuster was, except that from what Jason was saying, it must have carried movies—DVDs and such.

But it sounded more like a wrecking company. Yet even through his confusion, he recognized Jason's passion. And he remembered Jason's disdain for Walmart. Now he understood.

"And that…," Jason said, pointing through the windshield at a statue of a man standing high atop a pedestal at the end of the median where Main went from being a huge street down to only a lane in either direction. "That's our monument to a Union soldier. He used to have a rifle, but some jerk broke it with a golf ball. I don't know how he managed that, but that's the story. Statue has been there over a hundred years. Why would anyone do something like that? You know, when it was built, it only cost like a thousand dollars or something? And that giant pedestal? A hundred dollars. Talk about inflation!"

"Jason?" Adam asked, thinking about how very wide the street was behind them. "Your street back there. It is so wide." Wider than any street he'd ever seen in Monterosia. He wasn't sure Times Square was that wide, but it was hard to tell from pictures. "Why would a small town like ours be so wide?" Then he smiled. He realized he'd called Buckman "our town." The culture shock was receding and being replaced with something totally different.

"Oh!" Jason nodded. "People used to park their cars in the middle of the street. Diagonally. There are pictures at the Buckman museum." He rolled his eyes. "Yeah, I know. A town our size with a museum. But people are proud of their home, and it used to be quite the hopping place, I guess. There were two railroads that came through and a coal mine, and some wealthy people live here, not counting the Buckman that founded us. We can stop by the museum if you want."

For the next couple of hours they drove around, Jason pointing out the sights, such as they were. The Samson House—the museum Jason had mentioned. The elementary and high schools—Home of the Badgers. Go Badgers—which were across the street from each other. Deriddere, Inc. "They make the Roll & Step, a step stool used all over the country." Some of Buckman's nine churches, including his mother's United Methodist Church—and he'd eyed Adam knowingly over that one. Jason showed him the YMCA, where Adam discovered he could work out in the gym and go swimming. He loved to swim more than anything, and the possibility intrigued him. Later, when they drove by the town barbershop, Adam suggested they stop.

"Really?" Jason said.

"I could use a trim," Adam said. "Here"—he touched the sides of his head, then the back—"and here. Don't you think?"

"I love your hair. But can we save it for another day?"

"Sure," Adam said, thinking he could go alone later. He had watched many old American television shows, and the barbershop seemed like a center in small towns where one could talk and learn what was going on. Shouldn't he know what was going on in his town?

My town! What do you know?

"That," Jason said, pointing out a redbrick-and-whitewood building with a bronze stag rearing up on its hindquarters at one corner, "is the Wild Hunt. It's pretty pricey. People drive from all of the neighboring towns, so they can stay open even with their prices. American food."

"Which is?" Adam asked.

"Steak, baked chicken, trout, and catfish. And if you're lucky, venison. Do you eat deer in Italy?"

Adam sighed. "We do…."

"You don't like venison?" Jason asked. "It can be gamey tasting if it's not cooked right."

"My… family. It is a rite of manhood that we must go on our first hunt at thirteen. I had to go. And I had to make a kill. There was no choice." In fact, if he hadn't made the kill, hadn't gotten a deer, no one else in the country could hunt them either. He'd hated it. Hated killing the magnificent beast. Hated the whole day knowing that if he didn't bring one down that day, the consequences would be dire.

So he did it. Endured the blood being wiped on his face. Did not vomit when he drank some of the blood from a stag's-head chalice, and then ate the heart. Luckily the latter was cooked. His father wanted him to know that when he was a boy, he'd had to take a bite while it was fresh from the carcass and still warm.

When it was Cristiano's turn, he got his buck less than two hours after the hunters went out. His brother was so proud. Adam could only hope his father hadn't meant for him to overhear when he told Cristiano, "Perhaps you should have been heir!"

"I will eat venison. But because of my… history… I do not enjoy eating it. I cannot stop seeing that majestic animal in my scope. Its eyes wide. Its nostrils flaring. Rearing up. And then I killed it…." He trembled.

"God," Jason said. "I'm sorry. I didn't mean to bring up bad memories. And it's not like I can really afford to go there anyway."

Adam looked into the concern written on Jason's beautiful face and sighed, reached out, cupped his cheek, and apologized. "I didn't mean to bring us down. We are having a good time, yes?"

"Yes," Jason answered. "I know I am."

Adam tried to smile. And then he thought of something. Thought about Jason not being able to afford to eat at the Wild Hunt. And how he could. Maybe he should take him….

"Hey! Let's go to Pop's Drug & Soda. We can have an ice cream soda."

"I am not sure what that is," Adam admitted.

Jason's eyes flew wide. "Oh no! That's a crime. Let's take care of that right now."

Pop's Drug & Soda was a redbrick (of course), two-story building on Main Street, about halfway between The Briar Patch and the statue of the Union soldier. It sat on the corner and was rectangular and not connected to other buildings like so many were on Main. A red-and-forest-green sign stuck out from the building with Drug & Soda above and below that the red-on-white Coca-Cola logo. No mention of "Pop."

Outside, old men sat around a couple of tables playing checkers and chess.

"Hello, Mr. Chandler," Jason said to one of them, who raised a hand in return. "His wife makes the pies I sell at the Patch. They're flawless." Then to Mr. Chandler he said, "Tell Wilda I said hello."

"And you can tell her tomorrow when she delivers," Mr. Chandler said in return.

Jason nodded and held the door open for Adam.

Inside, a long counter with attached stools ran down almost the entire length of the room. Most of them were taken, mainly by paired-off teenagers drinking something milky or foamy from cone-shaped glassware. One or two were eating sandwiches that intrigued Adam's sense of smell and looked vaguely like the kind he'd seen on television for places with such silly names like

McDonald's and Burger King, and he'd seen nothing vaguely appetizing about what they had to offer.

And they were all over Italy and the rest of Europe, but there were none in Monterosia! Adam's father had refused their pleas to sell their "food" in his country. It was a matter of national pride, he would say. Salvestro said he enjoyed "hamburgers," but Adam had never been tempted to try them. They didn't look anything like ham, and with their "special sauce" dripping from them, he thought they even looked rather disgusting. But what he'd seen looked very little like what the kids here were eating. Pop's sandwiches were huge, thick things. Far more appealing than what he'd seen on TV.

"No school?" Adam asked quietly, pointing at the kids.

"They probably just got out."

Jason nodded to two empty seats next to each other.

Behind the counter were rows of big jars full of candy, and behind them were turnstiles of postcards, greeting cards, books (mostly games like sudoku and crossword puzzles)—

"So no competition," said Jason, nodding and smiling. "With the books."

—and various odds and ends like sunglasses and reading glasses, something called ChapStick, fingernail polish, combs, brushes, and folded maps. All of it was cheap.

In the back was another small counter going widthwise, and behind it, Adam was startled to see, was a mannequin wearing a white lab-style coat. It was smiling and giving a jaunty wave.

"That's Sam," Jason explained. "Pop's father. Back from the days when this *was* a drugstore."

"It's not anymore?" Adam asked.

"They just couldn't keep it going. I'm not sure exactly why. Changing times and more drugs I think. Prices...."

"Walmart?" Adam asked.

Jason shook his head. "No. Pop hasn't carried any modern drugs, or anything vaguely medicinal but aspirin and cough drops"—he pointed to the rotating stands—"for as long as *I* can remember. But you should check the display before we leave. Pop has one of the biggest collections of antique drugs and remedies around. You know, cure-alls, tonics, elixirs. There's even tapeworms!" He shuddered.

And Adam *didn't* know what Jason was talking about. Cure-alls? Tapeworms?

Pop, as it turned out, was a huge man, both in height and girth. He had sparkling blue eyes, a reddish nose, a ready smile, and graying hair combed over his bald head in some poor attempt to hide his lack of follicles on top. It was hard to guess his age. He could have been anywhere between fifty and his late sixties, or even older. His chubby face and jovial expression hid his age well. He wiped his hands on a white towel and greeted them with a "Good afternoon, boys. What'll it be?"

Adam turned to Jason, no idea how to answer.

Jason nodded eagerly. "You have to have a soda. What do you like? Chocolate? Strawberry? Or maybe you'd like a float?"

Adam could only look at Jason blankly. He didn't know what sodas or floats were. "I like chocolate," he said.

"Okay. Let's just start with the basics." He looked at Pop. "Two chocolate sodas." Then facing Adam again, he said, "We haven't eaten lunch. You hungry?"

"Yes, I am." Something smelled wonderful. He thought it was those sandwiches.

"Hamburger, then?"

Adam shrugged.

"You want yours with cheese?"

"I like cheese."

Jason gave a little laugh. "Of course you do. Two cheeseburgers as well, Pop. Sauté some onions. I want to spoil him for life on the best burgers he could ever try."

"Well, thank you for saying that," Pop said. "Fries with that?"

"Of course," Jason answered. "Can't have hamburgers without french fries."

Pop said, "Coming right up, then," and headed down to the other end of the counter and began working over a big open griddle, but not before he leaned toward Jason and said, "Good on you, Jason. He's quite the looker."

Jason turned back to Adam, blushing.

"What?" Adam asked.

Jason cleared his throat. "He says you're an attractive man."

"Oh." Adam sat back. "Is he gay *too*?" How many gay men lived in Buckman?

"Pop? No, I don't think so. But his grandson is. Pop and his son.... Well, his son left Buckman. I'm not sure why. It was all kind of sad, really. I don't know much, and I don't ask. Anyway, the son went to New York, or maybe LA, and came out as gay, then died of AIDS. But he had a kid somehow. I don't know that either. But now Pop is very supportive of the gay community and has even marched with PFLAG in Pride parades in Kansas City, or at least when they had them. Now he does AIDS Walk every year and raises quite a bit of money. I've sponsored him for something like five years now. My sister and my parents do too."

It was one of those places where Adam had to pause and think about what Jason had just said. Even though he was fluent in English, as well as Slovenian and French, there were things he had to think about to get. All right, LA was Los Angeles. But he had *no* idea what a "peaflag" was. He knew what AIDS was, of course, but was unfamiliar with the term AIDS Walk. It somehow raised money, though. Probably to help in AIDS research?

The hamburgers didn't take long, and in no time at all, Pop placed plates down before them with their food, including heaping piles of what looked like *patatine fritte*. He tried one of them first and—*oh, hot!*—it was pretty good. Crispy on the outside, golden good on the inside.

And now the *ham*burger.

He picked up the big sandwich and looked at Jason, who nodded encouragement. Adam studied it again. The meat was huge. As thick as his thumb held sideways. How was he supposed to open his mouth that much? Finally, he shrugged, opened wide, and took a bite.

And his mouth was almost immediately flooded by an explosion of flavor. The meat and onion and cheese and, God, *so* good! His jaws almost ached from it. Could you get a charley horse in your jaw? It seemed that you might.

He was looking up when Pop plunked their chocolate sodas down. They too seemed almost too big. Americans and their portions.

"Wipe your mouth," Jason said. "You've got juice from the burger all over." He giggled.

Adam grabbed up one of the big napkins and, embarrassed, wiped his mouth and was surprised to see how wet it was.

Then he saw that Jason was holding his glass. Now he was looking at him challengingly.

Adam took him up on it, picked up his glass, put the straw in his mouth, and sucked on it. At first nothing happened.

"The straw is stuck down in the ice cream," Jason explained. "Take the straw out, suck hard, and then put it back down the side of the glass."

So he did and tasted a little something cold and sweet, and when he took his second drink out of the glass, the sugary chocolate flavor hit him good and hard and wondrous.

"Bravissimo," he said, and Jason grinned.

After that, it was almost a contest to see who could keep consuming their food the fastest. Good. It was all so good.

Adam had to rest before he was done, though. Maybe stop altogether. He was quite frankly stuffed.

He looked at Jason and quite suddenly—he wasn't sure what had triggered it—he wanted to kiss Jason. Right there. Right then.

He laughed quietly and told Jason, and Jason said, "God. Please."

Adam looked over Jason's shoulder. "There are kids here...."

"They're not kids. They're teenagers. Maybe they'll be educated. I'm not asking you to suck my face off. Just a kiss. A quick, *real* kiss. Because we can. Please?"

Please? How could he refuse that? How could he refuse Jason anything? So he did it. He leaned in and closed his eyes and kissed him. Right there. Right then.

It wasn't a long kiss. It wasn't too short, either. A simple thing really. But as he pulled back, opened his eyes, and looked into Jason's, he knew it came with a promise.

Adam realized he wanted to take Jason to bed. Right then. Right that moment.

He didn't suggest it. Not yet. Not until he could be honest.

But he did realize something.

He was falling in love.

THE next week was a delight. They caught a baseball game and cheered on the Buckman Badgers as if it were the final game of the World Series and not simply a small-town high school team. It was that exciting.

Jason had Adam over for dinner, making both his Grandmother Brewster's chicken and his Grandma Higgs's biscuits. He seemed pretty confident Adam would love them both.

He did.

They went to see a scary movie, and they let out little gasps and screams, and they laughed and held hands and made out some too, because they were sitting in the back, and no one was watching them.

On Friday, Adam took Jason to the Wild Hunt and vowed he would find a way to tell Jason who he really was. He needed to. For lots of reasons, the biggest being that *not* telling him really had turned into some kind of lie. He thought that if he *could* tell Jason and Jason took it well, maybe tonight was the night they could make love for the first time. The idea was exciting and nerve-racking.

Jason was stunned when he saw where Adam was taking them and tried to object, to say it was too expensive, but Adam wouldn't listen. Insisted. Besides, he really didn't know what expensive was. He'd never had a budget until now, and for the most part was staying within it. Figured maybe he could find a little work from home. Thought he would do translations from English to Italian and back again. A lady across the street from him did the same with German, and she told him she'd get back with him on how he might find work. He mentioned it to Jason, who got quite excited and said that New Visions Press, his publisher, was just beginning a new venture by translating their books into other languages, and he thought Italian was one of them. This got Adam's mind to racing.

The owner of the Wild Hunt was a stocky but powerfully built man with a trim beard just starting to gray. He seemed to have caught on immediately that this was a romantic dinner and put them in a darkened corner. He brought them the bottle of wine Adam had ordered and opened it himself, even put it in an ice bucket.

There was indeed venison that night, but Adam didn't order it, and neither did Jason. They had fish instead. Monterosia was known for its seafood. Adam loved fish and thought he would try the trout, a fish he'd never had before. He found it was delicious. Jason had the catfish, and they shared. Adam loved their first meal-sharing experience. It brought out feelings he couldn't believe were growing so fast.

Adam opened his mouth half a dozen times that night to tell Jason who he was—what he was—but somehow it didn't happen. For one thing, Jason was in a mood Adam had not seen before. He was talking about writing and how in just the last two nights, it had taken off again. Suddenly— he blushed as he said it, and Adam could tell even by candlelight—it was easy to write romance again. That he could believe two men could magically find each other and fall in love in a world that was sometimes quite cold.

Adam delighted in Jason's delight, but it somehow kept him from revealing himself. That worried him.

What if Jason found out *before* he could tell him?

The next night they had dinner at Jason's family's home. He'd already been nervous, but the *not* telling Jason made him even more so. He couldn't help but feel that something big was about to happen. He could only hope he was ready.

Chapter Seventeen

JASON had been a nervous wreck before he and Adam got to his parents' house. He'd never brought a man home before. When he picked Adam up, his breath was taken away. Even so casual as being dressed in a plaid button-down shirt, jeans, and boat shoes without socks, Adam was elegant. As if he were a little... more than the common man. It was enough to conjure up all kinds of god stories again.

Any worries he may have had were banished the moment they arrived at the split-level ranch house where he was raised. He wasn't quite sure whether to let himself in or not, despite the fact that he'd done so a million, million times before. The decision was taken from him when the door opened just as they stepped up onto the porch above sidewalk level. It was his mother, no surprise, and she welcomed them and motioned them inside.

She hugged Jason in the foyer and asked if Adam hugged.

Adam did, awkward as it was with him holding two bottles of wine. He'd bought them earlier that day when they decided on a whim to track down the mysterious Silver Springs Winery early that morning. It had taken the entire day. Luckily Daphne had come to the rescue again. She reminded them that the bill was going to be high when it came due. It had been a marvelous day even though they realized they probably should have done it on a day when they could have stayed the night in Kansas City.

"I'm so glad you came," Jason's mother said and bizarrely seemed to *almost* curtsy. Jason had never seen her do anything like it in his life. And then seeing the bottles in Adam's hands, she said, "For me?"

"Ma certo," he said, giving a tiny bow himself. "Indeed. Jason said you liked reds, and we got you the merlot, which we were already in love with, and the Syrah, which I think is even better. A stunning difference for me."

Her eyes sparkled. "I'm sure I will enjoy them." Then, turning, she called out, "*Charlie*. The boys are here."

Jason looked to the right into the living room, and there was Dad, wearing a blue plaid shirt and jeans. Except for the shoes and the lacking socks, it was as if he and Adam had planned to match. He got out of his ancient recliner, hitched up his jeans, and came to join them. He noticed Adam's attire.

"I see you got the memo." With a hand movement, he indicated both of their shirts.

Adam might have been confused for about a second and then grinned and got into the game. "Sure," he exclaimed. "Of course I did."

Thank God!

"It was Jason here that didn't." He pointed at Jason's red-and-blue rugby shirt.

Jason laughed and was grateful Adam was handling all this so well. His father could be a little… weird at times. And at times, he and Daphne had wondered how their parents had ever happened. Their mother was one thing. Sometimes she seemed like Carol Brady from *The Brady Bunch*, but at others could transform into something akin to a force of nature, where all she was missing were sparks and flashes of electricity in her eyes. Her voice might be bright and cheerful and turn in no time to an earthy rumble, a growl of thunder.

Whereas Dad was just plain earthy. A guy. An often goofy guy, always cracking a joke, pulling one—like a joy buzzer or a spring snake flinging itself from a mock mixed-nuts can. It belied his intelligence and computer-like knowledge of almost anything. His passion for the planet. He'd gone to Earth Day events since some of the first in the very early seventies. He was a hippie without looking the least bit like one, but had Jason's parents been just a couple years older, he was sure they would have gone to Woodstock or placed flowers at the ends of gun barrels during the 1967 march outside the Pentagon to end the Vietnam War.

Whenever he and Daphne did wonder at what brought their parents together, they would remember those things. They would remember when *both* their mother *and* father went to Washington DC for Obama's inauguration or the Women's March in 2017, the largest single-day protest in US History.

They realized that was what had made their force-of-nature mother want to be with their humble father. And it made them proud to be their children and decide that Zeus didn't quite measure up to their sometimes nutty, but always heroic, and wonderfully *human* father.

But gods please, Jason prayed, *no joy buzzer*.

They shook then.

And there was no buzzer.

After that, the evening went beautifully.

ADAM had been pretty nervous. Pretty nervous? Hell! He'd been nauseous, his stomach like twisted lead. He'd met numerous dignitaries and diplomats, including President Barack Obama, who'd treated him as if Monterosia was a superpower that the world depended on for peace. He'd dedicated years of his life to visiting orphanages, the sick and aged and dying in hospitals and their homes not only throughout Monterosia, but all over Europe as well. He'd gone to important meetings, including the 2015 United Nations Climate Change Conference in Paris. And in Rome, he had once had a personal meeting with the pope. He not only convinced his father to give food to those who worked in the palace but also spend the money that was spent each year on the birthday celebrations for him and Cristiano on the poor instead, as well as establishing Boxing Day as an official national holiday. He had been instrumental in his father signing the treaty of the International Criminal Court. He established several charities to help the poor and fund AIDS and cancer research, donating and volunteering his time as well as using his charm to get many other influential people, as well as public figures, to donate money. He'd done all that and maintained his composure and made his family and country proud.

But meeting Jason's parents?

Gods!

He'd never been so anxious in his life.

Because it wasn't Amadeo Montefalcone, the prince of Monterosia, meeting the couple. It was just plain Adam Terranova—the heart of who he was. And even that was a mask.

Jason's mother—"Iris," she told him to call her. "After all, it's a bit early for you to call me Mom, right?"—took the wines to the kitchen while Charlie, Jason's father, led them to the backyard. And there was Daphne, the sister, and a big handsome gentleman, also in jeans and a plaid shirt.

"See," he said to Jason. "He got the memo too."

Charlie found this hilarious and went straight to Daphne's companion to loudly tell him about it. Laughter ensued. Daphne came to them, eyes sparkling, and asked them how their day went.

"*Oddio!*" he exclaimed, kissing his fingertips. "*Bellissimo!* And I cannot express how grateful I am for you giving us this day. I owe you a thousandfold!" He gave his slight bow.

"What he said," Jason added, his voice filled with emotion. It made Adam's heart happy. "You don't know. Was it busy?"

"Nothing I couldn't handle," she replied. "But I did make it a burger day."

"And I helped," said the boyfriend.

Jason's eyebrows shot up. "Really?"

"Really," Daphne supplied and looked up at the man with something very much like love in her eyes.

"Yup," the man said and held out his hand. "I'm Tom Rucker."

Adam shook it. Tom was a big man with big hands and a firm shake. Adam hoped he didn't disappoint Tom with his return squeeze and it measured up to his country strong test of masculinity. "Nice to meet you, Tom. I'm Adam Terranova."

Daphne and Jason apologized in unison for not introducing them, but he didn't mind, and Tom didn't seem to care either.

"I love making burgers and shit," he said. "I'm making them tonight!" He grinned a huge grin and cocked a thumb over to the big grill not far away.

Adam couldn't help but wonder how they would compare to Pop's.

"I'm sorry you have to have burgers twice a day," Jason said.

"Naw," Tom said. "I don't care. I love burgers."

"And besides," Daphne interjected, "he had meatloaf. I snagged the last two pieces out of your fridge, Jason. Hope you weren't saving them for something."

"Just you," he said.

After that, the evening went beautifully. Smoothly and as comfortable as could be. Adam had to fight tears once, watching this family. The way they moved together. Jason's parents and the obvious years between them. Daphne and Tom and the something budding between them. The way he served her food and the way she fetched a beer for him, and the staring and him looming over her as if to protect her. But most of all how these people accepted him here with their son and brother as if it were the most normal thing in the world for two men to be… well, together. At least, that is what he thought they were. This was more than just what the Americans called "hanging out," wasn't it?

He hoped so.

For some reason he hoped so with all his heart.

They played a game called basketball, which he had seen on television but had never played. The girls against the boys. He messed up several times but then started to get the hang of it and prayed he pulled his weight. It was very important that he prove himself to this family. The problem was that Daphne had what they called a deadly hook shot. Impossible to do anything about, or at least nearly so. In the end the girls won. Tom told him that of course they did. The men let them. "If we don't want to sleep on the couch."

He looked at Daphne with a sweet, possessive love, and she blushed and flashed a look at everyone, but if Iris or Charlie caught what Tom had said, they at least pretended not to. It wasn't long after that Jason and his sister went off to the side and giggled between themselves, little doubt about Tom's revelation. At the same time, Iris and Charlie had a quick conference, and then Charlie asked Tom for help in the kitchen cleaning up.

"Let me," Adam said.

"No," Iris said and motioned to the picnic table that had been big enough for all of them to eat comfortably with room for all the food. "I was wanting a little time with you, Adam. If you don't mind."

Ah. This is it, he thought. But just what would "it" be?

She held up her glass of wine. "First, the wine is excellent. Jason said you two spent the day driving to the winery and back?"

He nodded. "Good as bread," he said. It had turned out to be rather extraordinary. They'd spent every evening together doing things from meals to scary movies to simply looking up at the stars. But being in a car for over four hours one way, spending time at the winery doing tastings, and then the long drive back…? Well, that was different.

"Different experience being trapped in a car together, isn't it?" she asked as if reading his mind. "But good, I think. When you can't leave the room for a while, you notice things about each other that might have taken a lot longer otherwise. What did you notice?"

"That Jason smells nice," he said and then was startled he'd done it. He blushed.

"I take it you don't mean his cologne?" she asked. "Especially when he doesn't tend to wear it?"

He blushed all the more and nodded.

"Anything else?"

That was easy. "I like that he loves watching the country go by. So many people don't look, you know? Even when they can't really help it. They tune it all out. But Jason...." Adam smiled. "He... in my language I would say, *è tutto pepe*. It means he is all pepper."

She raised an eyebrow. "I take it that loses something in translation?"

He laughed. "I suppose. It is like... well, in cooking, pepper brings food up a note. Peppers bring out something in bland food. Infuse it with a richer flavor. Tantalizes the senses with greater aromas."

"Jason tantalizes you, does he?" she asked with an obviously bemused smile.

Now he blushed all the more.

"The saying means that he is full of life. His personality is so... what word...? Animated? Is that right?"

She gave an ever so slight a shrug. A "you tell me" without speaking.

He smiled. "*Stimolante!* We say it for someone who can challenge you to be better. Yes. It means he lifts you up. He lifts *me*."

Her eyebrow raised even more.

"Now you are just trying to embarrass me," he said. "I know you understand."

She nodded. "That pesky language barrier."

"Sì," he replied.

"Cultural differences," she continued.

He nodded.

"Between Buckman, Missouri, USA and Monterosia…."

Adam froze. He felt as if he had been turned to stone. Completely unable to move, he was so shocked. Had she really said that? Or had he misheard?

"I take it that means you haven't told him."

"I…. I…." The words wouldn't come out no matter how much his mouth worked.

"But you should, don't you think? I mean, since it seems you two are intent on each other and not just two horny young men. Do you have that word? Horny?"

Adam's mouth fell open. Then he somehow managed to nod. He knew what it meant. *Eccitato*. Sexually excited.

"Not that my son doesn't need a little sex. And stop being so shocked. You are both normal young men with sexual needs, and as far as I know—and Jason is pretty open with me—it has been a long time since he's been helped with those."

"I…. I…." Dammit! He couldn't talk!

"I'm being nosy enough to ask because you boys are spending a lot of time together, and it is obvious to me that he is developing feelings for you pretty fast."

"I… I am as well, Iris." God! He'd finally said something.

"Oh?"

He heard his father then, in his head. Telling him about Cupid's arrow. He gulped. "My father says that is how you know it is real. When it strikes swiftly." He smacked the left side of his chest. "Cupid's arrow. It almost *hurts*!"

"Your father the king?" She said it so matter-of-factly.

"How did you know?"

She chuckled. "You. You told me to look up Trieste, and I did, and that pulled up more information. How Monterosia wasn't letting anyone fly in or out for now because their prince had vanished off the face of the earth, and I clicked on that—because, hey, that's interesting—and there was a picture of a man who is your spitting image."

Merda! He had told her to look it up, hadn't he? And Jason had told him that she was a lifelong librarian. Of course she would look.

"You'll tell him?"

He swallowed hard. "I will, Iris. I have been trying to. Trying to find the words. It is a big thing, you know? What if he doesn't want a runaway prince in his life? But not telling him? I feel like I am lying."

"I agree. Because those first weeks when you get to know each other? If there are important things to say that you don't say? They get harder and harder. And I think knowing that you're a prince is a big thing."

"You're so... calm about it. This isn't an everyday thing, no?"

She smiled. Laughed a bit. "No. It certainly isn't."

"And how do you feel about your son... what do you say...? Dating a prince?"

"I think my son is lonely and needs love in his life, and as long as you're not a serial killer, I'm okay."

He swallowed again.

"But maybe now I'm leaving something out."

"Oh?" This was the most astonishing conversation! So calm.

"When I found out who you were, I looked up *who* you were."

"I.... What do you mean?" he asked.

"I looked up what kind of man you are…. You, Adam. And I found I liked him. Amadeo Montefalcone is an amazing, heroic man. I think Jason deserves a chance to get to know him. Don't you?"

Adam was stunned into silence once more. Tears blurred his vision.

And he found that he liked this woman very much.

So he promised.

Chapter Eighteen

"YOUR place or mine?" Jason asked in his big old pickup truck as they were leaving his parents' house.

"It doesn't really matter, does it?" Adam answered. "Park in the alley, and we will be at both places."

They laughed.

Then, "I sure would like to sit with all those candles on your back porch... ah... piazza."

Nice, Adam thought. "You really did like that, didn't you?"

Jason looked at him, and for a moment Adam could imagine what he'd looked like as a child. So sweet. Right now, his beautiful eyes, even with the only light being from the dashboard and the streetlamps... were so.... Trusting.

Which made him feel terrible.

I've got to do this.

But what if he's angry?

Things compound. It will only get worse the longer you wait.

"Let us light you some candles."

Jason grinned. In that moment, Adam knew—*knew*—he could look at Jason's smiles for the rest of his life. Conventional wisdom said it was crazy. But his father? His father said love was swift. Like Cupid's arrow to his heart. That it could hurt. And certainly, the idea of losing Jason hurt as much as an arrow in the heart must.

After Jason did indeed park his truck in the alley, off in the grass on his side, they walked the short distance—Jason took his hand, *Oddio!*—to his piazza. They went through the gate, and together they lit the candles. Soon it was the glowing wonderland it had been on that first real meal together, just the two of them. When the wonder had begun.

"Do you have any wine?" Jason asked.

Adam rolled his eyes. Ma dai. Really?

Jason was still looking at him, so he answered, "We have a case, *amore mio*."

And Jason rolled his eyes in turn. "Of course we do."

"Sit," Adam said. "I will get it." He went into the house, looked at the nearly full box they'd come home with, and picked out what he hoped was the right choice. The Syrah. It was getting late, and somehow the merlot was wrong and the moscato too sweet. And besides, the last needed to be chilled.

He brought it back and, standing, poured their glasses before turning around and setting up music for them. After all, it was said that music warmed the heart. Correct?

He turned around, and Jason was standing there looking like some kind of vision. His eyes sparkled in the candlelight, his dark hair emphasized his lovely creamy skin, and tonight he had allowed his jawline to go dark with the shadow of a beard. All Adam could think of was how much he wanted to take him into his arms. Kiss him. Feel his lips against his own, the sweet roughness of his beard touching the shadow of his. Would it be soft as velvet? Rougher, like sandpaper? And what would it feel like in other places?

"This song," Jason said quietly. "What is he saying?"

It was in Italian.

"Ah…." Adam listened. "'More Beautiful Than,'" he said. "It is by Eros Ramazzotti. You have heard of him, yes?"

"I don't think so," Jason said.

No? "Really? He is very popular in…." The lie almost slipped out. He almost said, "in my country." And it was time to stop lying. "He is very popular in Italy and most of Europe. He has done duets with Tina Turner and Cher. Many others. I thought you would know him."

Jason gave a slight shrug. "Maybe if I heard the duets. Sometimes you've heard of people you didn't know you've heard of. When I first started liking P!nk, I was really surprised to discover how many of her songs I already knew and didn't know they were her…."

Adam nodded. "Maybe. But this one…." He paused. Listened. Translated. Then he held out his arms. "Dance with me?"

Jason smiled. "It's a little fast."

"Like my heart," Adam said aloud. "Looking at you there."

Jason's eyes widened, and he sighed.

"Come to me, *speranza mia*…."

Jason let out another little gasp and took a step.

Adam motioned with his arms again. *Take them, Jason*, he beamed at his love, with all of his heart. *My hope. My dream.* "We will sway to every other beat, *va bene?*"

Jason stepped into his arms, and Adam placed one hand on his hip, drew him close. They began a slow sway. Jason got the every-other-beat almost immediately, and their bodies fit together, and Adam knew his body would so respond. He looked into Jason's eyes. Such beautiful eyes.

"What is he saying?" Jason asked. "The words…?"

"He is saying," Adam said quietly, nodding toward his iPod, "that he is not sure how it began. Their romance. But that their story is never ending. That their passion will never go away. That with each other… they lose a little sanity, and they share the same fantasy."

He pulled Jason a little closer. Loved the feel of him. And prayed to the gods that this would not be their last dance.

"He says that singing to his love is not enough, that his lover deserves so much more. But all I can offer is my words of love."

"Y-your words?" Jason asked, eyes shimmering.

I did say my words…. Adam sighed. "That even as the years go by, my desire for you is endless. I carry it in my heart. That thoughts of you wake me at night because of how much you excite me."

"Excite you?" Jason asked.

Adam began to grow hard, and as they shifted their weight, he could feel that Jason was as well. God, he wanted to take Jason to bed. But how could he until he told him the truth?

Venus, please, he prayed. *I love him so. Don't let him turn away from me….*

"You deserve so much from me," he continued to paraphrase. "But all I can really offer you are my words of love." He paused, the words and the dance. "And my honesty."

"Adam?" Jason asked, and Adam saw the concern in his eyes. "What…?"

"Something that I haven't told you. Something I *need* to tell you. I haven't been honest."

Now was it fear he saw in Jason's eyes?

"You're a spy…," he whispered.

Adam's head drew back. What? "A spy?"

"A priest?" Jason asked.

What? Priest? "You think I'm a priest?"

"That's what Daphne said…."

"She thinks I'm a priest?" He didn't know whether to laugh or what.

Jason slumped. "She said maybe you were a defrocked priest sent away by the Vatican."

"She said that?" Adam said. Then, "I'm not Catholic. We talked about—"

"But you also said you haven't been honest with me. God. Did you have an affair with a bishop and you had to run away?"

Now he really did almost laugh. Would have if not for how serious this was. "Did Daphne suggest that as well?" he asked. They had been talking about him. Was it bad they were talking like that? About who he was?

Jason trembled. "Oh no. You're married. P-please tell me you're not married." His eyes were desperate.

"Oh Jason, amore mio. No, no. Solo tu. Only you. There is only you…."

Relief in that face now. But still fear. "Then what?"

And it was out of his mouth before he knew it. "I am a prince…."

Now it was Jason's turn to pull back. "A what?"

"You have heard of Monterosia?"

More confusion. "Mont… ta… row…?"

"Monterosia," Adam said, clear and proud. "It is my country. I am not from Italy."

Still confusion. Jason had never heard of his country. Like a lot of the world. Adam sighed sadly. "Monterosia is a small country… my country… between Italy and Slovenia, and—"

"Oh. Sure." Jason nodded. "I was just confused there. I still am. You're not from Italy. You're from Monterosia, and…." He paused. Adam could see things happening in Jason's eyes. Thinking. Processing. And then, "Prince?"

Adam sighed and nodded.

"Wait…. Didn't I see something in the news? A prince of a small European country vanished recently, and…."

Adam saw it happen. Saw the realization hit him.

"Oh my God. You're him? You're the prince of Monterosia? And you're living in my backyard? And you're…." He trembled. "Y-your holding me in your arms, and…."

Adam smiled. And hoped.

And suddenly Jason was smiling. "Oh my God! That is…"

Yes? Adam wondered.

"…that is *fantastic*!"

JASON could hardly believe Adam's words.

A prince.

He suddenly felt like crying.

Adam. The man he was falling in love with. Was a prince? It was impossible. Wasn't it?

"You're a prince?"

Adam nodded. Cautiously?

"You really are a prince? A real live prince?"

Still holding Jason lightly, he nodded. He'd gone a bit... tense.

"The man I am falling in love with is a prince?"

Finally, Adam smiled. "Falling in love...?"

"Oh Adam. Wasn't that obvious?"

Adam shivered in his arms. "You mean that?"

"Yes!" Jason exclaimed. "I can't stop thinking about you. I'm dreaming about you...."

The shivers went away.

"I've dreamed for years that some eagle from Olympus would sweep down and take me away. That I would have some wonderful adventure." He pulled himself tight against Adam, "But the gods don't do that anymore, do they? But a prince?" Now there were tears in his eyes. "I've been falling in love with you since the second we met, Adam. With you. And finding out you're a prince?" He grinned. "Why, this is what Lois Lane felt like when she found out that Clark Kent was really Superman."

"Amadeo," Adam said.

"Amadeo?" Jason asked.

"My name," he said. "It is Amadeo. Montefalcone." It sounded like lyrics in his musical voice.

Goose bumps rushed over him. "Amadeo Montefalcone."

Adam nodded. *Amadeo* nodded.

"Amadeo," he whispered back. "My gorgeous, sweet, kind, wonderful Adam is also Amadeo." A tear spilled down his cheek. How could this be happening? It was like a fairy tale. "Amadeo." He trembled. "This is like a fairy tale."

"You love me?" Adam said.

"I do. I know it's crazy. I know I should question it. It's too fast, right? Now have I scared you off? Do you think I'm a weirdo?"

"Oh Jason," Adam cried and kissed him.

It was no gentle, soft kiss.

It was passion.

It was fire.

It was the kiss of the gods.

Amadeo opened his mouth to Jason, and Jason responded in kind. Tongues danced. Teeth clashed. They gasped. Clutched at each other. Grappled. Jason's cock had softened a bit while they talked, but now he went hard all over again. Adam's length against his was like steel, and it was torturously wonderful. They ground their cocks together, and it was all Jason could do not to cum right then. As if sensing it, Adam suddenly pulled away and swept him up in his arms. Jason put his arms around his neck. They kissed once more, and then Adam said, "I am taking you to my bed, my beautiful Ganymede."

"Oh God," Jason near sobbed. "Please, Adam. Amadeo. *Please*."

He did. Adam carried him effortlessly across the patio—the piazza—and somehow opened the door and swept into the house with him. Through the little kitchen and the newly repaired living room and into the house's only bedroom. The only bedroom they needed. Then he laid Jason down on the bed. It was the first time he'd seen the room, but he only had eyes for Adam.

Adam stood over him, panting, and Jason could see now the length of his cock through his jeans. A lust so profound swept through him that he made a sound he couldn't identify. Something like a gasp and a growl combined. He'd never wanted anything or anyone as he did right now.

Then to his shock, Adam left the room in a rush.

"Adam?" he called out. Then, "Amadeo?"

A moment later he was back, with a platter covered with flaming candles. He quickly placed them around the room and switched off the overhead light. Now the room was glowing, and his Apollo, his Zeus, looked otherworldly and impossibly gorgeous. Captivating. Bewitching.

Adam began to unbutton his shirt, revealing bit by bit a glorious smooth chest, muscles like an ancient heroic statue. It seemed like this couldn't really be happening. Like it was something from Jason's imagination. Something from a dream.

But then his dream threw off his shirt and crawled up the bed and on top of him and kissed him again. Hard. Demanding. Taking him with that kiss.

Then he was kissing Jason's eyes, his forehead, down his cheeks and his ears. He tickled those ears and then sucked on the lobes, and Jason gasped and arched up into this lover, this prince.

A prince!

Now Amadeo was kissing Jason's neck, licking, sucking it lightly, going down to the collar of his shirt. He growled. He leaned back and pulled Jason up and then the shirt off over his head in one quick motion. Tossed it off somewhere. Pushed Jason back down with a hand in the center of his chest.

He straddled Jason then, his mouth open and his eyes heavy lidded with desire. Hunger.

I'm not going to last, Jason thought. *He is going to touch me down there and that's it. I'm going to cum.*

That wouldn't stop anything, though. He reached out his arms. Beckoned Adam into them. Adam came. He all but fell on Jason, kissing him again and then quickly lifting him slightly so that his head fell back, and he sucked at Jason's neck, and Jason gasped. Cried out. Wanted to shout.

Now Adam was licking and sucking and nibbling and biting. His collarbone. His chest. His nipples. Throwing his arms over his head, pinning them and burying his face in Jason's armpits one at a time. Sucking at the dampness there. Jason thrust his crotch up into Adam's, trying to gain some kind of friction. Some way to relieve the fever sweeping through him. There had never been anything like this. Nothing like this with Tim. There *could* have been nothing like this with Timothy. And certainly not with his own hand.

Adam was a lover, making Jason's skin and body feel things they had never felt before. He tingled everywhere.

The kisses were going lower and lower now, down his chest and belly. Adam's tongue laved his belly button, inducing sighs and laughter.

And now… now Adam was pulling at his belt, tugging at the button of his jeans, yanking down the zipper, and the relief and frustration were overwhelming. The pressure of jeans that had grown too tight vanished, but it was frustrating now he had nothing to thrust up against.

Except, God! Adam's face. Adam had moved down his body and pressed his face against Jason's length to kiss and suck at his underwear-clad cock, and he thought he might just die from the magnificence of it all.

"Amadeo! You're going to make me cum!" he cried.

"No!" cried his lover. And he yanked at Jason's jeans and underwear, struggling to pull them off. "Raise your ass!" It was a command, and Jason obeyed until the clothes were down to his knees. Then Adam used his own knees to drive Jason's calves tightly together and make Jason thrust his groin upward.

And Adam was upon him. He sucked Jason into his mouth, and the wetness and the heat was too pleasurable, too wonderful. As he'd predicted his orgasm swept over and through him that quickly, and he was pumping himself into Jason's mouth. Cumming deliriously hard. Over and over. He felt as if his life were going into Adam's desperately sucking mouth.

Then it was over, and he collapsed and was near sobbing when he heard a sound that.... Was Adam crying? Was his Amadeo crying?

He looked down, somehow finding the strength to prop himself up, and saw that Adam was gazing up at him, and he was crying. "Adam?" he asked.

"Oh my Jason," Adam said. "Amore mio. Vita mia. Luce mia. Anima mia."

Now tears were trickling down Jason's face. "Oh Adam." He didn't know exactly what Adam had said, but the meaning came through somehow.

But then Adam made it clear. "Jason, you are my beloved. My life, my light, my soul...."

"Adam. Amadeo. Gods, I don't know what to call you...!"

Adam was crawling up his body now, and he said, "When we are here, together like this, call me Amadeo."

And as Amadeo took Jason back into his arms, Jason said, "My Amadeo. I love you. You are my love and light and soul."

They kissed then, and Jason could taste himself and knew that he wanted, needed, to taste Adam. His Amadeo. This must be complete. At least partially. Jason nudged at his chest and his lover—*my lover!*—took the meaning and rolled over, and Jason kicked at his shoes and jeans so they fell off at last, then rolled himself and began to undo Amadeo's jeans, to pull at the buttons.

He gasped when his lover's cock surged up through the V of his jeans. He wore no underwear and there, there was

Amadeo's cock. It looked huge, and the head was mostly covered with a lovely foreskin that showed the shape of the glans beneath. It was wet from want and need. His balls, in their silken sac, were nearly hairless. It was beautiful. "Your cock," Jason gasped. "So beautiful."

"Yours is," Amadeo said.

Amadeo. His name was poetry!

Jason reached out and took his lover's length in his grasp and lifted it away enough to kiss it—

"Oh gods!" cried Amadeo.

—and wet his lips from the growing thick moisture there at the tip, now running down the shaft's length.

"Jason! *Amante!*"

He drew in Amadeo's heady scent, and it was clean and musky and terribly sexy. He carefully took Amadeo's sac into his other hand, and it was so alive and warm—the scrotum like satin, the balls like eggs— and he gently pressed his face into them, between them, kissing them, licking them, sucking at the skin— *exquisite*—and carefully sucking one ball, then the other, into his mouth.

Amadeo's fingers were in his hair now, lightly then firmly, tangling then combing. He sighed. He moaned. "Oh my Jason, my love…."

Jason let the testicle slip from his mouth, and then he licked up the shaft, gathering the wetness, luxuriating in it. It was sweeter than he'd experienced before, salty but not bitter. He moaned. Licked more thoroughly, trying to capture it all, before reaching the top and sucking him in deep.

Now Adam was shouting, and his hands in Jason's hair became more insistent.

"Oh Jason! *Oh! Mi stai uccidendo di piacere!*"

Jason began to bob up and down on the shaft, and God, it was so wonderful. It had been so long. Doing something he loved, and this cock... this one... so perfect. Thick but not unmanageable. Long but not too much, not more than he could take, especially after he remembered how to fully relax and take this beautiful man in to the root. He grew almost faint from the pleasure of it.

"Jason! I am going to...!"

Of course he didn't stop, and an instant later Amadeo flooded his mouth. He had to keep swallowing to drink him down, and then to his shock, he realized he was cumming too. Again. He hadn't even known he was pressing against Amadeo's leg, but now he was swept up in a second orgasm, and he had never known anything like it.

Finally, they both finished. Amadeo slumped, Jason melted into him, and it was as if they had become one.

What would it be like when this man was inside him?

"Come here, amante," Amadeo said then, breaking the silence. "Before I fall asleep I want you in my arms."

Somehow Jason did as his lover asked—*My lover! Oh, please, you are my lover, right?*—and made his way up so they were face-to-face, and they kissed, lightly and sweetly, and Amadeo pulled him so that his face lay on Amadeo's chest, a pillow unlike any other.

"I should have made love to you the way you did to me," Jason said quietly.

"We have all our lives ahead of us."

Jason froze.

"We do, do we not, Jason? I have not misunderstood something?"

Jason lifted his face and looked into Adam's, his Amadeo's, and tears began again. "You haven't misunderstood anything, Amadeo."

"Then you are my lover now? Please, Jason. Tell me that you are."

"Of course I am. I am your cupbearer. Forever."

Amadeo smiled. "Thank the gods…."

Jason wasn't sure when he fell asleep after that.

Interlude

THE next months really were a fairy tale for them both.

They spent all their time together. Adam even helped at the Patch. And somehow, no one ever recognized him. Apparently Monterosia really meant nothing to Midwesterners in the huge United States. They didn't know the world around them the way Europe needed to, or at least a large part of it. They lived in a sort of oblivious meandering. At least in Buckman. That is what Adam saw. And despite the fact that he had revealed himself and his name—the one they used alone, especially when they made love—he felt like Adam in this new place, his new home.

They made lots of love.

Adam took Jason first. Jason was afraid he would do it wrong, and Adam chuckled at that and said

Faunus would show him. Bacchus would take delight in teaching him. Nature would take its course.

But Adam was first. They bought Adam a baseball cap at Walmart. It was black with a raised metal bat symbol. Adam took one look at it, turned to Jason with a terribly stern look on his face, and said, "I'm Batman."

Jason exploded into laughter. "You've heard of Batman in Monterosia."

"My dear, I think they've heard of Batman on the moon. Of course we call him L'uomo Pipistrello. Or the Italian translation does. But.... 'I'm L'uomo Pipistrello!' just doesn't have the same ring to it."

"Not at all," Jason said, dissolving into laughter.

They took a proper trip into Kansas City. Actually closed The Briar Patch for a few days. Caught a Royals game and drank bad beer and ate big hot dogs and cheered on their team, which won, and won well. They went to a gay bar called The Male Box, and it wasn't until they were back in bed and he was fucking Jason that he quite suddenly caught the American pun and what the name of the bar really meant. At first Jason didn't know what to make of his lover laughing in the middle of thrusting into him, but when Amadeo stopped and explained, he joined in the laughter and begged him to fill his box.

At the game, Jason caught Adam looking at Royals T-shirts, touching a baseball cap.

"No!" he said, perhaps a little too loudly.

Adam gave him a curious look. "Why?"

Jason pointed at the price tags. T-shirts for forty-five dollars. Jerseys for a hundred and fifty. And baseball caps going for no less than forty. "You can get them *much* cheaper at Walmart."

"The insidious Walmart?" Adam asked.

"Touché." Jason nodded. "Look, before we go home, we'll stop at a place called Kansas Sampler. They've got a great selection. *Much* better prices. Maybe we can get you another Batman cap, too."

"No. Something else. Spiderman perhaps?"

"Anything you want," Jason replied.

Adam, for the first time truly not thinking about what he was doing, reached around Jason and placed his hand on Jason's lower back. Pulled him close. "*Anything*?" he asked, voice heavy.

Jason laughed in delight. "That you already have, mister."

There was another reason they went to the city on the days they did. They also went to a clinic and got tested for HIV. It was surprisingly nerve-wracking for both of them, and their nurse assured them it was for everyone.

Adam knew it was possible he had been infected. He guessed from several years of internet usage that it wasn't a high risk. After his time with Salvestro back in college, his highest-risk behavior had been fucking two men, one without a condom. It had been stupid and done at a time where he had been horribly lonely, and his father had been pressing him to marry a woman from a good family, who had at the last second decreed she was marrying for love and saved him (and her) from an unhappy marriage. All the other times had been oral. He or the other man on their knees in a dirty alley, in the dark. That was supposed to be very low risk, but there were differing opinions, He was relieved to find out the clinic wouldn't let them be tested together.

It reminded him that he still had things to tell Jason. Wrestled with whether he would. He had a right to a private past, didn't he? But whenever he looked at

Jason, gazing at him with total trust, something curled inside him. Something as dark as the shame he felt at the way he had reached out for contact with other men. It wasn't so much that the acts had been done in anonymity. It was that he'd met his need for human contact in a way that brought him shame, but he went and did it anyway. There had been many offerings from men in the light of day. An ambassador who he was sure would have been discreet.

And it was more aligned with something a teacher had said to him once when he was trying to figure out how to ask the man if masturbation was a sin. When he couldn't bring himself to ask, the man had said, "Amadeo, this is a rule I live by. If I am not sure if something is right or wrong and I do it anyway, then it *is* wrong. For *me*."

Seeking out anonymous sex instead of love had been wrong. For *him*. And the driving need had impelled him to do it anyway.

JASON was pretty sure he was okay. He didn't think Tim could be HIV+. He'd never been fucked, right? At least back in those days? Of course, it wasn't the only way to get it. Plus, who knew? Maybe Tim had used needles. It all seemed so impossible, and Jason wanted to make sure that the impossible was indeed impossible. After all, a lot of impossible things had happened lately hadn't they? His lover—*his lover!*—was the prince of a European country that went back for hundreds of years. The Monterosian people claimed back to Roman times, and had legends to back it up. Adam had promised to tell him all about it.

They had reason to celebrate that night when the gods granted their prayers.

And shyly, over a gelato served in an area called the Country Club Plaza that was almost real gelato, they blushed and hinted and finally discussed making love that night without a condom.

"They say the only way to be sure that you do not contract this virus," Adam said, "is from not having sex at all, or monogamy. And Jason, I want no one but you."

Jason had beamed at that and told him that he didn't want to be with anyone else either. Both agreed not even with Timothy Jeske and had a laugh.

That night they got a room at the Meridian Hotel, which was not cheap, but this was special. The view was spectacular, and they ordered room service and sat before the windows naked and ate and then made love.

"Please, vita mia. Me first. You do not know how much I need it."

Jason smiled and rolled onto his back and held out his arms, and Adam sat up, kneeled beside him. "No. You misunderstand. I want you to be inside me first. I want you to cum inside me. I need this. You inside me, when you are no longer inside me. Still there."

Once more the poetry of the way Adam said things nearly brought him to tears. So that night, he took a man for the first time without a condom. It was without exception the most exquisite thing Jason had ever experienced. Condoms really were like taking a shower with a raincoat on. He'd never known how much pleasure they took away. It was so different. He came in moments. But thankfully he was so aroused he never lost his erection, and with Adam urging him on, Jason fucked him a second time without withdrawing. It had been even better.

They did not leave the room until the last possible second the next day, and Jason had Adam's seed left inside him as well. They couldn't stop smiling at each other the entire next day.

Before they returned to Buckman, they stopped to have coffee in a shop that Jason had read was one of the places to go in Kansas City. It was a different experience for each of them. Jason was shocked that they didn't serve sweeteners or milk. Adam said the coffee was still weak when he tasted Jason's. But he found the espresso was utterly divine. He got into a conversation with the owner of the shop, and the coffee talk almost went out of control.

And Jason got a little embarrassed.

It turned out that Bean, the owner, would give anything to taste the coffee Jason hadn't liked. That Monterosia had an exclusive contract on a bean from Ethiopia called Caffe Bottaio, from the barrel makers who used to pack the beans into barrels previously used for brandy. It wasn't as expensive as the stuff made from civet cat shit, but was far more exclusive. If you wanted to drink Caffe Bottaio, you had to go to Monterosia to drink it. And there was a strict limit to how much you could buy. Small personal amounts, and never industrial.

"Promise me," the owner said, "that the next time you come through Kansas City, you will bring me enough for a cup—just one cup! I will give you a bag of anything in the store. Two!"

"And I didn't like it," Jason said back in the car on their way home, and he blushed again.

"Ah well," Adam said. "We like what we like!"

Buckman began to see them for what they were. They went everywhere together, and only a small group thought of them as the "faggots." Most people, those not yet ready to join PFLAG, referred to them as two wonderful young men. Jason and his "friend," Adam. A few customers stopped coming to the Patch. But more new ones came, and it made them both smile when they saw the occasional male couple. Couples who had found some small way to come out in a small town.

"I guess we're the Harvey Milks of Buckman," Jason said and then had to explain to Adam who the activist was.

"I feel happy to be equated with this man in any way. But can we skip someone assassinating us?"

Jason agreed that was a fine idea.

One day, Adam came to Jason with a surprise. He had translated the first chapter of *Down from Olympus* into Italian.

Jason had been astonished.

"I had to make a few changes…."

"Changes?" Jason had asked, not sure how he felt about that. "What do you mean, changes?"

"There are things that just don't translate. You remember when I told you *fare troppi atti in commedia?* To make too many acts in a comedy? Well, there are American idioms that don't translate into Italian. You say here—" Adam found the spot and pointed it out. "—that the kids are pulling Stanley's leg. But we do not have that phrase in Italian. It would mean nothing to anyone who read it. We might say instead 'to take someone around.'"

"Take someone around?"

"Yes. And near the end you say that the outfit Dominic wears fits him to a T. This has no meaning in Italian. So instead I put that it fit him like a paintbrush."

"Like a paintbrush?" Jason burst into laughter.

"Yes. It fits you so perfectly it looks like it's been painted onto your body."

"Well I'll be…."

Adam shrugged. "I hope this doesn't bother you."

Jason let him know that it was the last thing it did. It delighted him. "And I'm sending it to Gail tonight!"

"She is your publisher."

Jason nodded. "If she likes it, maybe she would hire you to translate the whole book. Maybe other books too."

Adam smiled. "I admit that is a part of why I brought it to you."

Jason sent the chapter to Gail.

Two weeks later she contacted them and told them that Aida Polo, the Italian language coordinator, had loved what he did and indeed wanted to offer him a job.

It had been another night for celebration.

JASON met Cristiano. As much as he could on Skype. Cristiano Montefalcone. Prince after Amadeo. Head of security. *He's my age*, Jason thought. I run a bookstore and sort of restaurant, and he is the head of security for a country. A small one perhaps—less than a quarter of a million people, but a country all the same.

Cristiano was nice. Very nice. Enthusiastic to meet him. "So you are the man who has stolen by brother's heart."

"I don't know if I stole it. He seemed to give it pretty freely."

Cristiano laughed. A big "Ha!" And then he said to his brother, "I am not into men, my brother. But I recognize a pretty one when I see him."

That word again, Jason thought that night. *Pretty. As a girl?*

"Is his heart," Cristiano continued, "as lovely?"

"Yes. Yes, my brother." The two of them lapsed into Monterosian for a moment and then seemed to realize they were being rude. Jason was simply delighted that he'd picked up a word here and there out of what they were saying.

Cristiano focused his attention back to Jason. "You know he was… how do you say? *Smitten* with you from the beginning. The first glance."

"Really?" Jason asked with a grin and looked at Adam, who was blushing. "Really?"

"You know it is true," Adam said. "Dalla prima volta che ti ho visto, ogni volta che ti sono vicino resto senza fiato. È come se ogni cellula del mio corpo sapesse da sempre di appartenerti."

"Beeella," Cristiano gasped. He looked at Jason. "You *must* be something special!"

"What did you say?" Jason asked Adam, who was all but panting. Then to Cristiano, "What did he say?"

"Ah, but it can only really be said in the language of love. You should learn, yes? If you're going to be with my brother."

"What did he say?" Jason practically yelled.

"He said since the first time he saw you, every time he's near you, he's breathless. He says it is as if every single cell of his body has always known that it belongs to you."

It was Jason's turn to gasp. "My God."

He looked back at Adam. "It's true with me as well," Jason said, heart soaring. "I feel that for you."

"I hope so," Cristiano said. "Do not hurt my brother,"

"I don't intend to," Jason said. "I only want to make him happy."

"Allora…. That is good. Very good."

Cristiano turned his attention back to his brother. "Your letter relieved our parents… and upset Mother all the more. She's very worried about you, Amadeo."

Adam sighed. "Of course she is. She is our mother."

"She wants me to find you. Her patience will not last."

Adam gave a grunt, then told Cristiano that he loved him.

After they signed off, Jason asked Adam again, "Those beautiful words Cristiano said. Did you really say that?"

"I say all that and more." Adam stood and pulled Jason into his arms. "It is as if my mind couldn't work in its full capacity if I'm not with you. My feelings for you seem to me like the ones Adonis felt for Venus: an overwhelming burning passion and love that, even if I knew this would destroy me within forever, I would decide to go for it, to be with you, my love."

There was nothing for the two of them to do after that but make mad, passionate love....

ADAM'S translation of Jason's book went well. Whenever they were apart for some reason, Adam worked on it. He loved Jason's book. The romance. The poetry. He wanted to capture that. Make it available to a whole different people. Wanted them to love Jason's words, not his own.

But it was not only while he was on his own that he worked on the translation. Jason had taken a new and intense interest in his novel again. They might work side by side for hours, stopping when they were so tired they were seeing double, or when one of them was working on a love scene that heated them to the point where they needed the love to be real-life.

The one thing that Adam wished was that he had told Jason about his alley sex. Although it might have ruined everything. But he also knew the longer he waited, the worse it would be.

They did finally make it to the Samson House, a beautiful old home built 150 years earlier by one of Buckman's founding families and turned into a museum. Jason was even able to show Adam pictures of the old-fashioned cars parked side by side, counter parallel to Main and right down its middle. People crowded the streets.

"Was something going on when this picture was taken?" Adam asked. "It is *so* busy! You might think this was taken in some mighty metropolis and not just...."

"A tiny little town in the middle of nowhere?" Jason offered.

Adam wasn't sure if he had somehow offended Jason.

"Jason. My entire country is only 285 square kilometers. We are mostly villages. Less than a quarter-million people. The town below the palace, Roccaforte, has a population of ten thousand. I *know* small. I do not make fun. When Cristiano and I chose where I would live, we chose small on purpose. And I am coming to love this town. Of course, having you living here is my biggest love of all...."

The look on Jason's face told Adam it was the perfect thing to say.

But one of the most delightful things that was happening was that Jason was learning Italian from Adam.

"Does Monterosia not have its own language?" Jason asked.

"No. Not really, thank God. Although there are some subtle differences. Nuances?"

"Idioms?" Jason suggested.

Adam smiled. "Yes. For instance, we say, 'to slay the bull,' as the best victory we can achieve."

Jason nodded, smiled. "That story you told me. Of Theseus defeating the giant bull that enslaved the people who lived where Monterosia is now."

Adam nodded. "Yes. You remember." He got a troubled look then as a memory flashed to the surface of his mind. It did at times. But usually in a dream.

"Adam?"

"It is nothing," he said and pointed at a piece of paper taped to the stove.

"*Stuffa*," Jason said.

"*Stufa*," Adam corrected. "Close." He pointed at the piece of paper on the kitchen window.

"*Finestra*," Jason said.

"Good." Adam smiled. Adam's smiles were very encouraging.

"Now this!" He pointed at the kitchen door. The paper was gone. They'd taken it down yesterday.

Jason grimaced. Then closed his eyes. Adam waited anxiously while Jason struggled.

Then Jason opened his eyes and smiled. "*Porta*," he said. "Like portal. A lot of the words are so similar. But prettier. Sometimes, if I think about it for a moment, I can see them in my mind's eye." Jason bounced. "This is just like when Nettie taught Celie to read in *The Color Purple*."

"*The Color Purple*?"

"You haven't seen it?" Jason looked aghast.

Adam shook his head. "I do not think so."

That night, Jason showed Adam *The Color Purple*. Adam laughed. He cried. He loved it. Especially, the line that said, "See, Father. Even sinners got soul." It was a personal echo for Adam. And a powerful moment. He felt something slip away then—something bad—as the characters on the television screen sang, "God is trying to tell you something…." The bad was replaced by some inner smile and a hug. Maybe the gods he loved to hear about were trying to tell *him* something.

It was time to tell Jason. It wasn't easy, but he did it. He told him of dark alleyways in Paris. Kneeling before men whose faces he could not see and performing acts so incredibly personal and intimate. Of his shame. Even of the arrest and his brother saving him.

"I knew I liked your brother," Jason said, pulling Adam into his arms without so much as a grimace or a flinch. "Now I *love* him."

"*Scusami?*" He wondered what Jason meant.

Jason pulled back enough to look at Adam's face, his eyes shining with love. "I am so sorry you've carried this. This guilt." Jason shook his head. "I've come so close to doing something just like it. And had it been as long for me as it had for you, I very well might have done the same thing."

Jason told him about the guy he'd nearly had sex with at a rest area and the coworker at Deriddere and the muscle guy from the Buckman Summer Fun Days. How close he'd come.

"You didn't do it, though."

"I had family and support. You had to hide. It makes me so angry that the world is still that way. That you couldn't be you."

"Until now," Adam said. "Until you."

AND they realized they really were living a fairy tale.

But fairy tales come with ogres and evil witches and dragons. Jason and Adam hadn't had to face anything like that.

Everything was about to change.

Chapter Nineteen

THE Briar Patch was closed for the evening, and Adam had made dinner. A delicious salad this time, with pasta and olive oil and fish. It was fish they'd gotten the last time they'd been to the city, and although not fresh caught, Adam had been excited that they'd actually found sea bass, plus octopus from Monterosia.

"A guy ordered it flown in and never showed up," said the man from the market downtown. "I gotta sell it. I'll give you a deal."

They took it. The coincidence was just too surreal.

That evening, Adam had been feeling uneasy, and he figured using his cooking skills for his lover would help. It did.

They were halfway through their meal when the knock came at the door.

Adam froze. His stomach dropped.

"You okay?" Jason asked him.

"Don't answer it," Adam said, stiffly, quietly.

"Why?"

Adam didn't answer. Couldn't. What would he say?

"What if it's my sister? My mom? My…."

The knocked turned to pounding. Pounding that sounded as if were it to continue the door would come down.

"God," Jason cried. "Who could…?"

"Open up!" came the loud cry. "Or I most certainly will knock it down!"

"Adam! Who could that…? What are you doing?"

Adam had stood and was slowly approaching the front door.

The man on the other side filled the large window in the door without showing his face.

Huge, thought Adam. He reached for the doorknob.

"What are you doing?" cried Jason. "Don't do that!"

But it was too late. Adam had already answered.

"Your Highness," said the mountain at the door. He was so huge, so crude, he would not be able to walk through the door without ducking. Without turning sideways.

It was Maschione, the Bull. And while Adam thought of him most of the time as "Marco," he was one of the fiercest men in all of Monterosia. Adam was sure that could be said of most of Europe. One of his oldest teachers. The man who had taught him self-defense, sword fighting, and what he called Theseus's "scientific" wrestling. Who was said to have trained Montaedus, Monterosia's founding hero.

How was he here? How had he known Adam was…? Cristiano? Had he sent the Bull here? Or had him hidden away nearby the whole time?

But if he was here, then something must have happened....

"Your Highness," said Maschione, one of Monterosia's highest operatives. Bodyguard. Agent. Field commander. Assassin. "I need you to come with me immediately."

Adam's first instinct was to walk through the door without question. This was the Bull after all!

But then—

"Amadeo!" Jason cried, and he froze. Woke up. Took a step back. He could not see Maschione's eyes. He wore sunglasses, not all that different from the kind Adam had chosen when he first came to the States. Big. Covering more than eyes. Covering intention.

"Your Highness," Maschione repeated. "You *must* come with me."

"No." Adam shook his head. "I live here now. I don't have to come with you."

Suddenly the Bull looked angry. "What? After what's happened! You would stay here after what's happened?" The Bull reared up and filled the doorway, fists clenched.

Adam stood back, and not only from the intimidating size of this man. This *more* than a man.

Now why did he think that? And gods, that dim memory, flashing beneath dark waters.

"What happened?" came Jason's voice, as if he were a hundred feet away instead of mere inches.

The Bull growled.

Adam's head cleared.

"Answer him!" he ordered, "Tell him what it is that we should already know—but don't. What's happened?"

For a moment, the Bull seemed to get even bigger. And then.... Then he relaxed ever so little. "Can it be you do not know? It has been on the television."

"We don't watch much television."

"Then I regret to inform you, Your Highness, that your father…."

Adam stiffened. Regret? Regret to inform? His father? "What about my father?" he cried.

"The King… he's had a heart attack. And they do not know if he will survive the night."

Adam stayed frozen for an impossible moment. What? Father? Heart attack. Might not survive the night?

And then he remembered *who he was*.

He was Amadeo Montefalcone, the prince and heir to the throne of Monterosia. And his place was at his father's side. He snapped his head in Jason's direction. "Jason," he said, "please prepare our bags. A few changes of clothes. Nothing more. All that we will truly need will be—"

"Not *him*," said the Bull.

Amadeo glared at Maschione. "*Yes*, him. This is Jason Evander Brewster. This is my heart and my soul. He *will* accompany us to my hearth."

"By the orders of your mother, the Queen Caterina Gianna Montefalcone, she has told me to only bring *you*."

"Then I will find my own way home. And when I get there, I will explain that you failed in your duty to the throne!"

The Bull stepped back, clearly surprised. "Your Highness."

"And if I am too late, where shall my mother direct her wrath?"

"But she said I *am* to take you home with all speed!"

"And did she tell you not to bring my love?"

"She said she worried that your companion might make your father's weak heart all the more fragile."

"Then he does not need to know, at present, that Jason is going with me, does he?"

"I… I…."

"And remember further, Maschione, that all too soon, *I* might sit on the throne." It was rough, but the man needed to be reminded. The Bull took a step back.

"Yes, Your Highness. But there is something else. A reason you can't go alone. The reason we *must* go *now*."

"Yes?"

"There is a news van on its way here. That television show. *Entertainment News*…."

"*Santo cielo*," Adam hissed.

"Today's Entertainment News."

"*Ma dai*," he muttered.

He could hear the program's motto in his head. *Be a TEN!* Jason had to explain to him what it meant. On a scale of one to ten, ten was the best. Of course. He realized he was familiar with the phrase. They claimed to be a ten, and if you watched them, that made *you* a ten. And of course it was also an acronym of the name of the show.

"Basta, Marco!" Adam ordered Maschione. "Not one more word! I know who they are!"

Adam turned to Jason. "My love. Quick. Prepare yourself a bag. We leave now."

It was only then that he saw Jason's expression. His countenance. His entire demeanor. He looked terrified.

JASON was terrified. Frozen. He could barely speak.

Adam wanted him to pack a bag and head to Monterosia? Just like that? Right now? How could he expect him to do that? There was his family. The Patch.

"Jason?"

Jason found he was trembling. And couldn't stop.

Adam stepped up to him, his eyes filled with concern. "Jason," he said again.

Jason looked up at him, opened his mouth to speak. But nothing came out.

"I—I can't go with you to Monterosia," he finally managed to say.

"Of course you can," Adam said. So sure. Unwavering.

He stammered words about his family. About The Briar Patch.

"Your family will be fine. The Briar Patch will be just fine."

"I don't have a passport!" he cried. Yes! That was it.

"You don't need it," the giant said. The one Adam called the Bull.

Jason looked from him back to Adam then back to the Bull again. Suddenly and completely, he understood what Richard Adams meant in his book *Watership Down*. When a rabbit would "go tharn." Become frozen in place when it saw the headlights of an oncoming car and could do nothing. Not make a sound. Not move.

"Jason."

They died.

He had to... to *un*tharn! But what Adam was asking him to do! It was impossible.

"There," said the Bull. "That is the love of your life! *Pffft*. That is who you left family and country behind to find. Frocio...."

"Marco!" Adam roared. "*Come osi! How dare* you!"

And that was what did it. It was in that word.

Frocio. He did not know what it meant. It was not a word on a piece of paper that Adam pointed to and asked him to repeat. But he could hear it in the man's voice. Faggot. Cocksucker.

It was in Adam's anger.

It was in Adam's unwavering knowledge that he would go with him. That he was Adam's love. His amore. His luce. His *per sempre*.

"Amadeo," he whispered, knowing there was no way he would hear him. But to his surprise, his lover immediately turned back.

"Jason?"

"Amadeo... I'm...."

"You are afraid?"

Jason nodded.

"*I* am afraid," his Amadeo said. "But I must go. This is my father. And Jason, amore mio—"

Amore mio. *My love.*

"—I can be courageous if you are at my side."

Something happened then. Something deep inside of him. Something changed. And even though this was a dark time—the darkest—somehow it felt like a spark—no, a shaft of light coming through... shining down on him.

"Luce mia...," Jason whispered.

Amadeo smiled. Placed a hand on his face, cupping it. "Tesoro mio... vita mia... amore mio...."

"Yes. I will come with you."

"Sicuro? You are sure?"

"I've never been so sure of anything in my life."

How could he not?

Chapter Twenty

THEY caught a small plane from a local airport and arrived at Kansas City International Airport faster than Jason would have thought possible.

From there they caught a rented private jet.

He never did pack a bag.

"Don't you think we have clothes in Monterosia?" said Maschione the Bull.

They did grab their toothbrushes.

And a shirt and shorts Jason had left on Adam's— Amadeo's—floor.

From now on he was Amadeo. How could he be anything, any*one*, else?

They sat together on a comfortable couch, Amadeo holding Jason. Jason thought it should be the other way around, but that was how he wanted it.

"I am sure your father will be all right," Jason assured him. "Heart attacks these days.... They're nothing."

Amadeo did not answer. Only held him.

And when he got up to go to the bathroom, the Bull stopped him. Placed a huge hand on his shoulder. Gave it a gentle squeeze. "I apologize to you, Jason Brewster. The word I used. It is ugly. I did not mean it. I hoped to anger you. Bring out your spirit. Your...."

"Bull?" Jason asked.

The huge man smiled. "Yes."

"It worked," Jason said.

"Yes," he said. "And Mr. Brewster...?"

"*Jason*," he told him.

The Bull gave a bow of his head. "And I am Marco Sebastiano. Maschione the Bull. Brother to the Minotaur. Bodyguard to the King."

"But now the prince."

Marco Sebastiano gave another bow, this one bigger.

"How long have you been in Buckman?" he asked.

A slight smile.

"Yes," Amadeo said, joining them. "How long?"

"Since the beginning, Your Highness."

Amadeo arched an eyebrow. "Cristiano?"

Another nod.

"You've been watching me?"

"Watching over you," Marco said.

"Where were you?" Jason asked. "How did we miss you?"

"The apartment over the barbershop."

Both their eyebrows shot up. The barbershop? Why, it wasn't much more than a block away from The Briar Patch.

"But how did you get around?" Jason wanted to know. He was so huge. "People would talk about someone like you."

Marco turned slightly and motioned to a man sitting quietly in an upright recliner down the way. A man that Jason had hardly noticed. Silent. Reserved. Nondescript.

Of course.

The kind of man you see and don't see.

"Mario Rossi," Adam said then. "There the whole time? And I never saw you."

And now a memory. Why, he'd been in the Patch!

"You've been in…."

The man nodded and turned back to his newspaper.

"Whoa…" was all Jason could say to that. *I didn't even notice him, and I should have purely from the fact that I didn't know him…!*

Jason somehow got Amadeo to eat. Assured him constantly that his father would be fine.

But Marco pulled him aside later.

Marco wasn't as sure.

THEY arrived in Monterosia early the next afternoon. The view as they flew in was spectacular. Gorgeous. The cliffs. The countryside. And they flew almost directly over the palace on their way to the nearby landing strip.

It wasn't anything like what Jason had imagined.

The castle sat atop a mighty pillar of rock that jutted out from a major cliff face. Except that pillar hardly seemed an adequate word. But the rounded shape fit. The structure itself looked more like a fortress, with mustard-colored walls and a red roof. Its only nod to the castles of fairy tales were the crenellations on several short towers that looked like a giant child had taken them from a palace and placed them randomly on top. There were numerous windows, and he could only hope they somehow let the sunshine in.

He'd imagined something like the Tower of London, Neuschwanstein Castle in Bavaria or even Caernarfon Castle in Wales, built by King Edward I. Instead he got a yellow fort. And he supposed that knowing those castles and anything about them once more confirmed his nerdiness. But what was there to do about that? The bread was the bread and the wine was the wine. Wait. Was he misusing that idiom?

"At last," Amadeo said, watching beside him. "My home. My *birth* home."

"It's very…." How to finish that comment?

"Yellow?" asked Amadeo. "If they make me take the crown, my first act will be to paint it."

"You cannot!" cried Marco Sebastiano.

"Watch me," said Amadeo. But not without a smile.

They were met at the plane by a 1932 Bugatti Type 41 Royale. Jason didn't know that of course, but he knew elegance. Long and sleek, blue and yellow-gold, with interior seating for, what? Two, three people? And then a space for the driver and one other outside and in front of the passenger section. Stunning.

"It belonged to my great-grandfather," Amadeo explained absently. "It has been kept in pristine condition ever since."

Amadeo took Jason in the back with him, and Marco Sebastiano all but filled the front, giving the driver very little room. The man didn't argue.

Twenty minutes later they reached the town of Roccaforte, which Jason learned was one of the largest in the country. With it came a hospital. And to Jason's relief, Montefalcone Ospedale didn't look like something out of another century, but quite modern.

"It is our main hospital," Amadeo explained. "There are clinics and such in the countryside of course. I imagine this is where my father will have his operation."

Marco opened the door for them. Men in black-and-blue uniforms swept out from the modern vehicles that had followed them on the drive, and it was then that Jason really saw it. The way Amadeo was holding himself now. The way he strode ahead. Royalty. In that moment he saw that this was real. When Amadeo told him he was a prince, it was still a fairy tale. Marco showing up and the plane and even the castle. He must have been numb somehow through that. But Amadeo's very bearing now said he was a prince.

Jason hurried after him—followed him as Amadeo followed the doctors who had dashed to greet him—down a long hall to a set of elevator banks. All too quickly they reached their destination. As they stepped out, one of the men who'd accompanied them placed a hand on Amadeo's arm.

"Perhaps His Highness should... go in alone?"

Amadeo glared at him, and he stood back.

"Maybe he's right?" Jason ventured. "This isn't about me. It's not about you being proud of me. It's about your father."

Amadeo smiled ever so slightly. Touched him on the hip. "I love you, Jason. You *are* my family. Please, I ask you. Come with me."

And so he did.

THE room they entered could have been any hospital room in any city in the world. There was nothing about it that was any different from the one Jason had visited when his aunt died. Then one he'd stayed in a few nights when he'd had pneumonia as a kid—although that was a long time ago, and it was hard to remember.

The woman who rose to great them, though, was exceptional. She had brown hair swept back from her face and held by some kind of clasp. Her eyes were a warm brown and were filled with guarded emotion. Jason wouldn't have known she was a queen had he seen her on the streets of Buckman. She wasn't wearing a gown or an ermine-trimmed cape or even a crown. But he would have known there was something about her. She stood as Amadeo did now. Head high. She radiated who she was. Her eyes were for her son, for this was obviously Amadeo's mother. Who else could she be?

"Amadeo, figlio mio," she said to Amadeo. "Sei qui. Sei qui, finalmente …. *Grazie a Dio!*"

"Mother," Amadeo said. He hesitated a moment, looking at the big man in the bed. But then he went to her and took her into his arms. "Madre. Sono qui."

Jason was surprised how much of their exchange he'd picked up. Madre. Mother. He thought it was "I'm here." And the things she'd said to him. Amadeo, my son. And something about thank God he was there at last.

"Figlio mio, my son. You are here just in time. He…. He has finally stabilized. They are taking him into surgery soon."

They held each other a long moment—

"Where is Cristiano?"

"He will be here soon. He is addressing the people. I cannot. I should, but I cannot."

—and there was nothing for Jason to say, to do. Except maybe step closer to the man on the bed? The man who must be Amadeo's father. A heavy man, asleep, pale. He didn't look well. How could he?

"Padre…."

Jason looked to see Amadeo standing beside him, looking down at his father with longing and love.

"Padre, sono qui. Perdonami." He fell to his knees, took his father's hand—it was a big hand—pressed his forehead to it. "I am here, my father."

Jason glanced past him and he saw Amadeo's mother. Looking at him. Assessing him. Judging him? Then she said to her son, "Amadeo. He cannot hear you. He has been this way for hours. Since last night."

"He hears me, Mother," Adam said. "He hears me."

And then, to their surprise…

"AM…. Amadeo…." It was a whisper. Rough. Dry. But when Adam looked up, his father's eyes were open. And looking at him.

His heavy heart felt hope in that instant. And it was so very heavy. To see the man who had raised him like this. The powerhouse brought to bed. The Rock of Monterosia brought so low.

"My son," his father said. "My b-beautiful son."

"Padre," he said, heart spreading with joy.

"My son" came the raspy voice. "You came…."

"Of course I did!"

"Proud of you, son…."

"Proud of me?" What had he said? Proud?

"For doing… what you did. Leaving…."

His mother gave a gasp behind him.

"It was brave. Do not… let anyone tell you differently. I wish sometimes I had had the… same courage. But I did… what I had to do…."

The words stunned Amadeo. As did the effort it took his father to say them. He looked so weak. "Rest, Father."

"I was waiting. I...." His father gasped for breath. "I did not want...."

"Father," Amadeo pleaded. "Do not speak. Rest."

"No...!" he said with a surprising amount of force. "There is.... Something I must say...."

Several medical personnel came in then. "Excuse me. But it is time. We want to operate now." He felt a hand on his shoulder. It squeezed. "Please, Your Highness."

Amadeo started to rise, but his father grabbed at his hand. The energy it must have taken. Amadeo dropped back down.

"Father?"

"Closer...," his beloved father said.

Amadeo leaned in.

"Do not face the bull," he whispered. "They will try and get you to. Your mother." He drew in a long, rattling gasp. "You... do not... know. You are not... p-prepared."

"Father?" The bull? Did he say the bull?

"I... I am an old man."

"No," Amadeo tried to say.

But before he could: "This may be my... time. If God wills it. If the doctors succeed, so... so be it." He squeezed Amadeo's hand with surprising strength. "Let it be.... What the gods decree."

"*Please*, Your Highness," said the man behind him, and then Marco was there, pulling him to his feet.

"They must take him now," Marco said.

Amadeo nodded.

But his father was still looking at him. He nodded. "What the gods decree," he whispered. "Do... you... hear?"

Amadeo nodded.

And then they took his father away.

Chapter Twenty-One

"AND now all we can do is pray," said Amadeo.

"Amen" came a voice, and Jason turned to see Cristiano, Amadeo's brother. Almost as beautiful as Amadeo, but not, of course. The Skype screen, with him in the dark, had not done him justice.

He's my age, Jason thought, not for the first time. *And he's the head of security for a nation, even if it is small.*

"Is it done?" the mother asked.

"It is. And as Amadeo has said, all there is to do is pray. And I have asked our people to do just that. As soon as the bishop is done leading that prayer, he will be here."

She gave a nod, almost as if she hadn't heard him, and looked intently at Amadeo, and then at Marco, who had just entered the room.

"Mother," Amadeo said. "I need you to meet someone. Someone very special to me."

Jason's stomach turned into a flock of butterflies as she looked back at Amadeo. Again almost as if she hadn't heard. But then her mind must be totally on her husband, Jason thought.

"*Hmm…?*" she said, a quiet sound.

With a hand to her back, Amadeo turned her slightly to face Jason, and the butterflies turned to stone.

"This is Jason Evander Brewster."

She looked at him, eyes distant. But then they focused with crystal clarity. "The someone special to you?" she asked.

"Yes." He turned to Jason. "Jason. This is my mother. Caterina Gianna Montefalcone, queen of Monterosia."

Jason bowed. He wasn't sure how to do it. But he did. He almost went to one knee. "I am most honored, Your Majesty." And when did he stand up straight?

He dared glance up and saw Amadeo nod. So he stood.

"This is the man you went to find?" she asked.

Jason couldn't help but see the surprise on Amadeo's face. His lover paused. Then said, voice only slightly unsteady, "Y-yes, Mother." Then stronger. "This is he."

She gave him a steady look then. But it was a look filled with many things. Jason wasn't sure if he might turn to gold or stone.

Finally she said, "I wish the times were different, Jason Evander Brewster. That we could talk. But now is not that time."

He bowed again. But when he looked up, she was still staring at him. Head raised a little higher. But eyes still *on* him.

"I do have a question, though, young man."

"Of course!" he all but blurted.

"Jason is a common enough name in your country, no?"

"Yes," Jason said. "I mean, it is."

"But Evander? Not so, I believe? Evander. I know it from legend. He was from Greece. And he brought the Greek gods, laws, and even alphabet to Italy, where he founded the city of Pallantium, which would one day become a part of Rome."

"Yes, ma'am." Ma'am? Did you call a queen ma'am? "Your Majesty," he said, taking no chances. "My mother. She named me after him and Jason of the Argonauts. She loves mythology. She named my sister Diana Daphne."

The queen pursed her lips. Then nodded. Was that the tiniest hint of a smile in her eyes, if not on those full lips? "That is good. The heroes should not be forgotten."

She turned back to her son. "Amadeo. There is something I must talk to you about immediately. It cannot wait."

"Yes, Mother?"

"You say that now all we can do for your father is to pray?"

"Yes, Mother."

"You are *wrong*. There *is* something else that can be done. And you, my son, are the only one who can do it."

Interlude

IT was crazy.

Completely crazy.

Things did not happen like this today. This was the twenty-first century. What his mother was suggesting…. It was something out of another time. *Pazzesco!* Something crazy!

She wanted him to fight the Bull of Monterosia?

Crazy! And he told her so.

"I don't understand," said Jason, who by all of Monterosia's traditions shouldn't have been there to have it explained.

"He stays," Amadeo said. "If you want me to listen to this foolishness, then you explain while he is here to advise me."

His mother hadn't known much. Wasn't supposed to know as much as she did. But then Father broke rules all the time, didn't he?

Something about a fight. With the legendary, mythological beast from mythology.

For legend said that Pasiphaë did not have one monstrous child... but two.

"Pasiphaë," Jason said. "She was the mother to the Minotaur, right? Poseidon gave Minos this amazing bull that he was supposed to sacrifice to the gods, but he didn't. So Poseidon made his wife fall in love with it and she... well... ah... she and the bull had a child. The Minotaur."

Amadeo stopped. "You never cease to amaze me."

"I told you I was a nerd."

Amadeo only shook his head. "Yes, you are right about the Minotaur. But what we in Monterosia know is that there were *two* children of Pasiphaë and the great white bull of Poseidon. She saved it. Had it sent away to be raised in a tiny village by good women—three women said to be the kindest mothers in the world. But this thing, it could not be anything other than it was. Its true nature came out, and it conquered the people there."

"The ancestors of Monterosia," Jason said.

"Exactly." They had talked about this once.

"And your mother.... She wants you to fight this thing? I don't understand!"

But then his mother didn't either. Not exactly. She knew more than she was supposed to. But not the whole story. It was Marco Sebastiano who explained it. Glaring at Jason, he explained.

"It is our oldest and most secret tradition," Marco said. "Going back to our oldest days. Whenever our people are in trouble, then our leader, whoever he may be, fights the Minotaur in a great ritual. He takes on the role of Montaedus, offspring of Illyrius, our all-but-forgotten hero, and another takes on the role of the Bull, and they fight. They have a ferocious fight. And if the hero wins, then Monterosia is saved."

It was then that a strange memory came back. And gods…. A dream. A dream of his father pushing at the head of the bull statue. Of going down that corridor hewn into the rock beneath the castle….

"Yes. It comes back to you now, doesn't it?" Marco said.

Amadeo looked up, stunned. "It was real?"

"You followed your father—"

"Down into some kind of pit." The images were coming back to him now. Torches. The tunnel opening up into a large cavern. Except it wasn't entirely a cavern. Man had helped make it. There were seats carved into the stone. Statues along the walls, some of them cut from the living rock.

"You saw the ritual. You saw your father fight the Bull."

"My God," Amadeo said, stunned. He saw it now. The firelight. The men. All of them nearly naked, wearing only loincloths. His father, the same. How surprised he'd been to see that even as an older man, he was muscle. All muscle. It was the first time he'd ever seen his father's bare chest, let alone his nearly naked body. And…

"Gods!"

"What is it?" Jason asked, leaping to his feet, color draining from his face.

"My father. I saw it. He fought another man. With a bull's head. Oh, it scared me. And I hid. Terrified that I would be found. By then there was no way for me to sneak away. More men had come in behind me…."

Marco nodded. "But you must have fallen asleep. And so we gave you a little wine laced with ancient herbs. And you forgot. *All* but forgot."

"I was around fourteen," he told Jason.

"It was 2003," Marco said. "Some of the worst droughts to hit Europe in hundreds of years. A heatwave that killed 70,000 people. Nearly 13,000 in Spain and Italy. We were losing many. Our vineyards, so important to our financial survival, even our ports that supply coffee throughout Europe, were affected. We almost lost our exclusive contract with Ethiopia, without which Caffe Bottaio, one of the most exclusive and sought-after coffees in the world, would not exist. We were a dying country. That is until your father fought the bull of Monterosia…."

"My God," said Amadeo. "It's like something out of a movie. A fairy tale."

"Or myth. But it is true. Shortly after that battle, the weather began to change. Monterosia was saved. And it happened so many times before. When Austria tried to conquer us. They beat so many, but not a tiny country like ours? Didn't you ever wonder about that?"

"I… I can't believe it."

"You know it is true," Marco said. "And now that your father is under the knife, *you* represent Monterosia. You are its leader. And you must fight the Bull."

"And that—" Amadeo saw it now. Clearly. "—would be you."

"You can't be serious!" Jason cried when they were left alone. When Amadeo commanded that Marco leave them alone. "You can't fight him! You can't! He'll kill you!"

"Surely it isn't real," Amadeo said. "It's a ritual, right? Like the one you told me about the two men who dress up as the Oak King and Holly King and wrestle for who wins the Summer and Winter Solstices. They know ahead of time who is going to win."

Jason looked at him, eyes wide, and trembling. "You're serious about this?"

And suddenly Amadeo knew. He was completely serious.

Chapter Twenty-Two

THEY took him down into the depths of Monterosia, deep in the rock, foundation of the palace. He was dressed in nothing but a loincloth and cape, and when they reached the temple, the great ritual room, they removed even that. Already men were there. Men he had known or been familiar with all his life. Noble men. Teachers. There was his brother Cristiano, looking almost as afraid as he felt. And there! Gods.... Even the bishop! All were dressed as he was. The room smelled of burning pitch and smoke and sweat. He was taken down an aisle in the three rows of rock seat to a round area, a miniature arena, no more than six meters.

The bishop himself walked into the center of the arena. He wore some type of collar, much like an Egyptian pharaoh's but without all the jewels. It was made of leather, and carved into its surface were a man and a bull, facing each other.

"Since time began for our people, this battle has taken place. Today, our Prince Amadeo becomes Montaedus, hero of Monterosia. And today he fights… the Bull!"

And to Amado's surprise, the bishop stepped out of the ring, and Marco Sebastiano came charging toward him out of the dark.

JASON had been forbidden to come.

Forbidden to be there when his lover, Adam, Amadeo, fought in ritual battle to save his father.

"You think this will save your father's life?" he'd asked Amadeo.

"I think it will." A soft smile came to his mouth. Then his eyes… they seemed to glow. He placed his hands on Jason's shoulders, looked into his eyes, and said, "I think maybe you might believe it is possible too."

"Why?" Why would Amadeo think such a thing?

"Because we have discussed this. The possibility of… gods. You are the namesake of Jason of the Argonauts. You have a statue of Ganymede and Zeus in your bedroom. You believe my mother leaves offerings to Juno to watch over my brother and me."

Well, yes. But it was all in fun, right? Nothing serious. But…

"But you mean this *for real*," he said. "This isn't something fun. It's not 'what if?' It's not an epic poem. It's not a—"

"Fairy tale?" Amadeo asked. "But haven't we agreed that we are living a fairy tale?"

That is when it happened. That was when he knew. Perhaps it wasn't real. Maybe it was just some kind of… placebo for the Monterosian people.

But wasn't there, hadn't there always been, a part of him that suspected more?

That maybe it was all real?

And if they thought he was going to miss it, to not be there, then the people of Monterosia were crazy.

It didn't take him long to find the bull statue.

And it didn't him long to find the way to open it....

AMADEO barely missed the charge. He stepped out of the way and heard the *whoosh* of Marco's fist pass by his head. Gods! What was this?

Marco turned.

No wonder the man had terrified Amadeo as a young man. Marco Sebastiano really was *huge*. The clothes he always wore somehow shrank him a bit. But now? With bare and glistening muscles? Now he was a giant. And that bull head. So real! Surely it was just a stuffed head, but he thought he could almost see the nostrils flare as Marco snorted. Marco.

The man-bull let out a bellow and charged again. Once more Amadeo only just sidestepped him, and now he was realizing, *I have no weapon. It's just me! How am I going to defeat this man? This is Maschione the Bull, Brother to the Minotaur. Bodyguard to the King!*

And again he came! At seeming twice the speed, and this time his fist did graze Amadeo's side as he leapt to avoid him. Oh the pain! It sent him spinning to the side and almost into the laps of the men in the first row.

The crowd moaned and cried out. He heard Cristiano above them all.

And they all cheered him on!

The next time Amadeo ducked instead of diving away, and as Marco went over him, he rose with all his might, punching up with both fists into Marco's belly. He heard Marco's breath rush out of him, but it had been almost like punching stone. Pain flared in his hands, and he wondered if he had broken bones.

Clearly this battle was getting too serious, too soon. This was supposed to be ritual, wasn't it?

"Amadeo!" shouted Marco. Then, "Montaedus!" For wasn't he Maschione the Bull? "Do you think this is a game? Do you think the gods would give favor to the kings of time if this was only a game? This is not a game! This is real. I am going to kill you! The gods insist that I try!"

The bull charged again. This time his fist—to Amadeo's shock—clipped him on the side of the head, and he spun like a top and collapsed on the ground. His ears were roaring from the pain, his eyes all but blinded by it.

And he came on again.

There was nothing he could do. Amadeo couldn't even focus.

He was going to die.

"Amadeo," he dimly heard Cristiano shout, as if from some far country, warm and safe and away from here.

Except then, in the greatest shock of all, Jason ran into the arena—

"No!" Jason cried.

—and took the charge.

His body folded like a snapped twig, and he was flung high into the air and into the dark.

"No!" Amadeo screamed and was up. Up on his feet.

The bull came back. But in that very instant, something happened.

Amadeo remembered. Remembered his training. And quite suddenly he knew why he had been trained in Theseus's "scientific" wrestling.

It was for this moment.

This time when Marco charged, he sprang up at the last second and caught the horns of the beast. He used the energy of that charge to fling himself up and over the creature's head. And at this moment, that is what Marco was. A creature. The bull.

The room cheered.

Once more, screaming now, the bull came back, arms and fists swinging. To no avail. Amadeo—*Montaedus*—did it again. He grabbed the horns. Flipped high into the air. A complete somersault. And landed on the beast's back. With all his strength, he locked on and began to pummel Maschione's side and neck. He was sure he was breaking bones. But the mask… or whatever it was… was thick. To reach the nerve ending he'd been taught to go for required something far more than grace and subtlety.

Then, just as he thought he wouldn't be able to do it, he felt it. Felt it give. Felt it give like a knot in Jason's back when he rubbed the day's cares away. But it was so much more. Something *big*. He felt it go. Almost heard it. Did hear Maschione shriek.

And then he collapsed. A great heap of man and muscle and bull.

The people roared.

But he barely heard it.

For he knew only one thing. He had to find Jason.

Chapter Twenty-Three

JASON was alive. In the hospital. But alive. And just across the hall from Amadeo's father. His very alive father.

Several of the bones in Amadeo's hands were broken. There was a cast. He had a concussion and was told to rest in a bed of his own. But he couldn't. He went back and forth between the bedsides of his father and his lover.

Jason came to, asking for him, and thank God he was there when he did. Amadeo took him delicately in his arms and held him and told him he loved him and covered his face with kisses.

And his father?

"You shouldn't have," he said. "I think it was maybe my time. Time to give up the throne."

"But Father. You have to rule. Because you know I cannot. And Cristiano is not ready…."

"What?" his brother said, who was there, of course, along with Mother. "Me?"

Amadeo turned to him. "Of course, my brother. I can't take the throne. Even if I could take Jason as my husband, even if the people allowed it, I have to have a legitimate offspring. Some surrogate mother would not do. Maybe one day. But not today. And let's be real. I could never take the crown. It was always yours."

"*No*, my brother," Cristiano objected. "I have always sworn my allegiance to you."

"But tell me you didn't wish for it."

"No," Cristiano cried. "I would never covet what is rightfully yours. I swore. I swore!"

"You never allowed yourself to covet the crown. Because you are who you are. But you know it as well as I do." He turned to his mother. "You know." His father. "You know it too."

"The—the people love you, Amadeo. You would make a great king."

Amadeo shook his head. "No. An adequate one, perhaps. But never a *great* king. That—" He turned back to Cristiano. "—that would be my brother. He should have been born first. The crown should have always been his."

Then Cristiano stepped up to him. Took Amadeo's forearms in his hands in the ancient way. "No. I should not have been born first. But if I could be a great king, it would only be because you were my older brother."

They moved into each other's arms and held on tight. For the longest time. And when they pulled back, Amadeo looked at his father. "I hereby abdica—"

His father held up a hand. "Wait. Remember *I* am the king. *I* decide."

It was not what Amadeo expected. His words froze in his open mouth.

"First I must ask you something."

His face. His father's face…. So serious!

"Y-yes Father?"

"This Jason…."

Amadeo's heart swelled. And stopped at the same time. "Yes, Father?"

An infinite pause.

Finally…

"You love him."

"Oh Father. With all my heart. All my being."

"Was it fast?" his father asked then.

"Fast, Father?"

"Was it Cupid's arrow to your heart?" He swiftly brought his hand to his chest.

Amadeo winced. Saw his father had not struck himself. Just a symbol. He smiled. "Oh yes, Father." He struck his own chest. But hard. Because he could. *Grazie Dio*. "It almost hurt!"

"Did you fall into his eyes?"

"I fell into his eyes and then into love."

His father smiled. "Then you know." Eyes brimming.

And now Amadeo too was ready to cry.

"I *know*," he said.

"Then so be it," his father said.

After that, all there was to do was go to Jason and tell him the news.

Chapter Twenty-Four

IT was the first Monterosian wedding on television. The world watched. A royal wedding. A royal wedding between two men.

Dignitaries from most of the world were there, although the President of the United States begged off.

Jason didn't care. His parents were there. His sister was there.

She was part of the wedding. "I'd better be!" So she had strewn flowers petals. She didn't care as long as she was a part of it.

There was great fanfare and magazine articles and anger and cheers and love, love, love. Because in the end, love wins. Always.

Any fears Amadeo may have had to how his people would react were needless. In the weeks after they had both recovered from their injuries in the pit, Amadeo had taken Jason all over his country, the way Jason had shown him his town of Buckman. And of course, Jason had charmed everyone wherever they went. He was Jason after all. They were careful not to display what they were to each other. They were discreet. But when the word came out—and it would have to if they wanted to marry—they found that people had seen it anyway.

"How could you not?" was the kind of thing people said. "The love shining in their eyes for each other! *Bellissimo!*"

The people had seen their love, and it mattered not. They only wanted their prince to be happy.

In years to come, Monterosia would become one of the biggest European tourist attractions for gay, lesbian, and transgender people from all over the world.

A year after the wedding, Monterosia had its first Gay Pride. Thousands of people came. The hotels filled, and then there were no rooms in the inns, and the people had to—no, they willingly—opened their homes. They did not know the details of the secret ritual of the battle of Montaedus and Maschione the Bull. Not the *details*. But they knew that their beloved prince might have died if it were not for Jason Brewster, and soon they came to love him as well.

The wedding was held in the great Episcopal Church in Roccaforte. The bishop presided.

Changes were made in the classic ceremony. For instance, both men came up the aisle together.

"Is this really happening?" Jason asked as they stood in the back of the huge church in the instant before they were to begin their walk.

"Of course it is, il mio amore," Amadeo said. "It's a fairy tale."

The music began.

And so did their happily ever after.

Special Thanks

FIRST and foremost, to Emanuela Piasentini, Ugo Telese, Lily Carpenetti, and Giuliana Demontis. They tirelessly answered my questions about all things Italian. Any mistakes made herein are mine and not theirs.

Elin Gregory (as usual—see book dedication!), without whose help the county of Monterosia simply wouldn't exist.

And to Kim Fielding, who further expanded my understanding of the region where my Monterosia exists. Thank you so very much for that and more, Kim!

And also to:

Noah Willoughby for countless hours of transcribing and research. Another who was instrumental in the creation of Monterosia. He came up with its flag!

C.L. Miles for so much editing, and of course for Tom "Rucker."

Amanda Clay, the librarian, for book suggestions and absolutely for sure, the Roll & Step, and a ton of other stuff as well.

Arshad Ahsanuddin for "faded-bloodstain brown." LOL!

MJ O'Shea for Kit Harrington.

Christopher Floyd for Ian Harding.

Carl Bucholz for the Badgers.

Jean A Stuntz for "Today's Entertainment News"— Be a TEN!

Michela Biasca, Ugo Telese, and Sara Benatti for helping me understand how Italians feel about American coffee.

To Lucy Watson Campbell, Rory Ni Coileain, Pauline Johnson, Alicia Nordwell, and Noah Willoughby for helping name the people of Buckman.

And finally, and not to be forgotten(!), to my editors—Andi, Nicole, and Susan—who make me shine. I love you!

Coming in October 2018

DREAMSPUN DESIRES

Dreamspun Desires #67
The Spy's Love Song by Kim Fielding

For a singer and a spy, love might be mission impossible.

Jaxon Powers has what most only dream of. Fame. Fortune. Gold records and Grammy awards. Lavish hotel suites and an endless parade of eager bedmates. He's adored all over the world—even in the remote, repressive country of Vasnytsia, where the tyrannical dictator is a big fan. The State Department hopes a performance might improve US relations with a dangerous enemy. But it means Jaxon's going in alone… with one exception.

Secret agent Reid Stanfill has a covert agenda with global ramifications. Duty means everything to him, even when it involves protecting a jaded rock star. Jaxon and Reid's mutual attraction is dangerous under Vasnytsia's harsh laws—and matters get even worse when they're trapped inside the borders. Romance will have to wait… assuming they make it out alive.

Dreamspun Desires #68
Handle With Care by Cari Z.

A fragile heart needs extra care.

Burned-out social worker Aaron McCoy is on vacation for the first time in years—boss's orders. Road-tripping to his brother's wedding with his best friend, Tyler, seems a fun way to spend the mandatory two-week leave, and they set out for Kansas—and a difficult homecoming.

Aaron's mother was a drug addict, and his adorable younger brother was quickly adopted, while Aaron spent his childhood in foster care. As Aaron mends fences, Tyler hopes to show him that this time, he won't be left behind to face his problems alone.

Aaron's opening up to how right it feels to be with Tyler and to the possibility of taking the leap from friends to lovers. But along with the wedding celebration comes a painful reminder of the past. Aaron's heart is still breakable. Can he put it in Tyler's hands?